DESPERATE ESCAPE

A slug whizzed past my shoulder. The next one took my horse in the neck. A fountain of blood sprayed Zeb as he pulled his horse side by side with mine. I grabbed Zeb's shoulders and he spurred the black, pulling me onto his horse behind him. A bullet spun my hat away.

The sheriff was eight or ten yards ahead, still on the sidewalk. We had no choice: we'd have to ride directly past him. His face was a crimson mask and his mouth was moving rapidly. He was trying to feed another round into his 30.06, and the lever was obviously jammed. He was tugging and pulling and cursing and, suddenly, he was moving the butt of the rifle to his shoulder.

"Use your gun!" Stone yelled. "I'm empty!"

I drew my pistol....

PARTNERS

PAUL BAGDON

LEISURE BOOKS NEW YORK CITY

A LEISURE BOOK®

January 2006

Published by

Dorchester Publishing Co., Inc.
200 Madison Avenue
New York, NY 10016

ISBN 0-8439-5669-0

The name "Leisure Books" and the stylized "L" with design are trademarks of Dorchester Publishing Co., Inc.

Printed in the United States of America.

Visit us on the web at www.dorchesterpub.com.

PARTNERS

Chapter One

When a man has walked almost twenty-five miles in two days in temperatures so hot even the damned rattlers and prairie dogs are afraid to leave cover after noon without sun bonnets, I'd say that man has every right on God's sweet earth to be a bit testy.

Further, when that same gentleman has had the finest piece of horseflesh he ever rode shot out from under him, and been robbed of almost everything he owned except his saddle, I'd be willing to grant that he deserved to irritable and out of sorts, so to speak.

All that could well be the reason Zeb Stone knocked me silly in the middle of Main Street in Burnt Rock, Texas, at noon on July 17, 1883.

I'd been sitting on the wooden bench in the shade in front of the Drover Inn, watching a sleek, black ant try to carry a piece of dried horse apple twice his size across the wooden sidewalk. I was also giving no little serious thought as to how I could scrape together the price of a taste of red-eye and a cold beer, when I took notice of the little cloud of dust Zeb was stirring

1

into the air as he walked. I quit overseeing the ant and his piece of horse apple and focused on Zeb, instead. I'll say one thing for the man: He was one hell of a walker. He took long, swinging strides as if he was in a big hurry, and his right arm and hand moved as precisely as the pendulum in a twenty-dollar Regulator clock. The tips of his fingers almost—but not quite—grazed the empty holster that hung low on his right thigh, tied securely in place with a piece of latigo.

I had some time to look Zeb Stone over closely, as I wasn't about to go out under that sun until I had to. I saw that he was tall, but not as tall as he initially appeared. I figured that he gave the impression of height because he moved somewhat stiffly, as does a soldier in a drill formation, and because his back was rifle barrel straight. Zeb was dressed much like any other cowpuncher or drifter: a beat-to-hell hat with its brim shaped and rolled to both keep the sun out of his eyes and let the rain run off; a gray work shirt that hadn't been new for a long, long time; crusty, dust-colored denim pants that had once been blue; and a pair of scuffed and worn boots with high, riding heels. His face was a mask of sweat, grit, and beard stubble.

When Zeb was about twenty feet from me, I pasted a big smile on my face and loped over to him, my right hand extended in front of me, all ready to shake with him.

"Good afternoon, friend," I said, all gracious and affable, "welcome to Burnt Rock. Our little town isn't much to look at, but it certainly beats hell out of the desert. Say—how about this: We'll go on over to the

Drover and you can set us up to a little something to cut the dust? My name's Pound . . ."

Zeb Stone stopped, shifted the raggedy-assed stock saddle he'd been carrying on his right shoulder to his left, and hit me so hard and so fast with his right hand that I never even saw the punch coming. Folks tell me I was out for the better part of ten minutes. Folks also tell me that Zeb stepped over me, marched to the trough in front of the Drover and climbed into it, boots, pants, gunbelt, shirt, hat, and all, and sucked enough of that murky, scum-green water to lower the depth in the trough a solid inch.

When I finally came to, I was stretched out on my back on the dirt-and-sawdust floor of the Drover Inn. I knew where I was right off. I'd been there—in the same position—more than a few times before. Zeb Stone, still dripping wet from the trough, with pieces of slime and crud stirred up from the bottom sticking to him, was hunkered next to me. When he saw I was conscious, he nodded at me, grinning.

"I'm Zeb Stone," he said. "You 'bout ready for that drink?"

The cowhands and merchants who had been standing around gawking down at me saw I wasn't going to die or do anything else spectacular, and they drifted back to the bar and the poker tables. Stone put his hand out to me and I took it, and together we got me to my feet. My legs were shaky, but I managed to hobble to a table and drop into one of the splintery, uneven-legged chairs. Stone sat in the other and began wrestling and cursing his right boot off his foot. It was quite a battle. His feet must have done a good bit of swelling as he walked all those miles.

"Son—of—a—bitch," he grunted through clenched teeth, "here—she—comes!" He hauled the boot free and held it over the table by its heel. Four double eagles clattered onto the rough, booze-soaked surface. Stone pushed three of the coins into his pocket and walked to the bar—leaving his boot on the table— with the other. When he came back, he carried a tray with a full bottle of whiskey and six or eight schooners of beer on it. He listed sharply to his right side but didn't spill a drop of his precious cargo. My jaw didn't hurt nearly as much as I thought it did when Stone set the tray on the table next to his boot. He grinned again and said, "Let's get to it, Mr. Pound."

A cowboy passing by laughed at the "Mister" part. I glared at him but didn't say anything. Zeb Stone and I, as he so kindly suggested, got to it.

The level of the rusty-tasting liquor in the bottle had dropped well below the halfway mark, and Stone had been back to the bar several times to have the mugs refilled with beer. There hadn't been a great deal of conversation. I told Zeb about Burnt Rock, which didn't take long at all.

Finally, between swallows, I asked, "Why'd you clout me, Zeb?"

"Well, Mr. Pound," he said after considering the question fo a moment, "I guess because you was the only one there." He thought for another moment. "Yeah. Because I needed to lay into someone and you was the only one around. Nothin' personal in it.

Now, lemme ask you a question: How come you talk so funny?"

"Talk funny? I don't know what—"

"Yeah," Stone interrupted. "You don't say 'ain't' and you don't cuss, and before I whacked you, you said, 'Good afternoon, friend,' 'stead of just 'Howdy.' Why's that?"

Stone's eyes—a deep blue—showed only interest. He wasn't making sport of me at all. That was clear to me.

I drained a beer. "I am—was—a schoolteacher. Perhaps—"

"There! That's what I mean. I can't recollect ever hearin' anybody say 'perhaps' before, 'cept maybe a preacher or a politician or some such." Zeb took a solid slug from the bottle. "You say you *was* a schoolteacher. Ain't you one no more, Mr. Pound?"

"No," I answered. "I'm not. The good citizens of Burnt Rock hired me a year ago, but fired me after a month because they felt I was somewhat prone to take a drink."

"Would you be a booze hound, Mr. Pound?"

"Absolutely," I said. "Absolutely. By the way, my name isn't actually Pound. It's Lawrence Basil Taylor. I've always used L. B. Taylor as my legal signature. When I first came to Burnt Rock, the imbecile who runs and owns the boardinghouse thought I was abbreviating the word 'pound' with my first two initials and entered me in his book as 'Pound' Taylor. The schoolchildren and townspeople and cowboys picked up on that and the name stuck. I've been Pound ever since."

Zeb thought that over. "Well. Damn. But Pound is a good a name as any, ain't it?"

"I suppose so," I answered. I was beginning to worry. Although there were several fresh beers on the tray, the liquor was almost gone.

"You wan' 'nother bottle, Pound?"

My fear whooshed out in a long and grateful sigh.

"Most definitely, Zeb. Most definitely."

Halfway through our second bottle, I asked Zeb how he happened to be walking into Burnt Rock carrying a saddle, and why he'd been in such a foul humor.

"It's like this," he said. "I'd been traveling west and I ran smack into the town of One Flag. I got into a poker game that lasted damn near three days. I won better'n two hundred dollars in cash, a Sharps buffalo rifle, one of them copper arthuritis bracelets . . ."

"Arthritis," I said, "not arthuritis."

Stone eyed me for a bit and then went on. "I always heard it arthuritis. Anyway, I was dealt a handful of cow pie and slivers, but I bluffed my way right onto the back of the damnedest Appaloosa stud horse you've ever seen. He was pretty enough to bring tears to a man's eyes. When the game finally busted up, I was so tired I could hardly stand, but I figured I'd better put some miles between me an' One Flag. I'd been playin' a straight, honest game—hardly cheatin' at all—but lots of them locals ain't happy when a stranger cleans them out. So I tossed my saddle on the Appy, gave the crow-bait I'd been riding to a kid on the street, and started riding. I didn't push my new horse for speed, but I kept him movin' steady for a night and a day before we holed up at a stop on the stage line. I slept in the saddle a lot, but that Appy, he just kept movin'. We rested up at the coach stop for a day an' then lit out again. The second day after that, I was dozin' in my saddle when my horse's head up an' exploded an' he went straight down. I hit hard and kept still, not moving. I whacked my head on a hunk of rock pretty good an' I was bleedin' steady. That's what saved me, I guess. Them three riders who done in my horse figured the fall croaked me. They took everything—money, Sharps, arthuritis bracelet, an' my Colt. My saddle an' gunbelt an' boots wasn't worth anything, so they left them. They missed the double eagles I walk on." He shook his head slowly, sadly, from side to side. "My Colt, though—she was a beauty. I had bone grips on her, and I filed the front sight level so it wouldn't snag in my holster." He sighed. "I could shoot the feelers off a grasshopper at a hundred paces with that iron. But I'll tell you this, Pound: I seen all three of those men, an' one day I'll see them again an' settle up."

An ordinary cowpuncher has no particular use for a pistol such as Stone described. My curiosity got the best of me. "What is it you do for a living, Zeb?" I asked.

Stone set his beer mug on the table and leaned forward. His eyes met and locked with mine.

"I'm a shootist," he said quietly.

"Hired?"

"Of *course* hired. I said I was a shootist, not some gun-crazy kid." He paused a moment. "You got any objections to drinkin' with a hired gun, Pound?"

"None," I said. "None at all."

7

Stone sat back and relaxed. "You do that a lot," he said.

"Do what a lot?"

"Use the same word twice in a row. Like absolutely . . . an', uhh . . . definitely . . . an' just now, none. Why's that, Pound?"

"Beats me," I said. Then I added, "Beats me," and laughed along with my new friend.

My memory of the rest of that day and night tapers off right about there. I have a vague recollection of leaving the Drover with Zeb and another bottle, and it seems to me that we ate something somewhere along Main Street, but I'm not sure about that.

The early-morning sun, already flexing its muscles, dragged me from unconsciousness. Zeb and I had passed out behind the blacksmith shop and stable. I was feeling extremely poorly until I pushed myself up into a sitting position and saw that the bottle—our third? fourth?—still contained a couple of inches of whiskey. I drained it, glad that it was in a bottle. I couldn't have handled a glass with my trembling hands. In a few minutes, my shakes and headache were gone.

Zeb's snoring sounded like a warped and rusty saw trying to cut steel. He was stretched out on his back, clutching his right boot to his chest, much in the fashion in which a young girl holds her favorite doll as she sleeps. Apparently, Zeb had carried the boot with him all night rather than try to pull it back onto his swollen foot. His saddle was a couple of feet away. I took a long, careful look at Zeb as he slept. He couldn't have been a day older than twenty-five. Damn, I thought, he's almost twenty years younger than I am. Why that made any difference or struck me as being important, I don't know. But it did. I nudged his shoulder with the empty bottle. The tempo of his snoring became ragged and uneven as he awakened. He struggled his way up to a sitting position and shook his head. Both of those moves were major mistakes.

"Sweet, Holy God," he said hoarsely. His lips were parched and cracked, and the waft of his breath that I caught could have peeled whitewash from a pigsty. He rubbed at his eyes with the backs of his hands and then tried to focus on me.

"Pound?" he croaked.

"What, Zeb?"

"I'm hurtin' real bad. Any whiskey left?"

"Nope. We drank it all last night. I could use a little taste myself, but . . ."

Stone closed his eyes and held his boot in my direction. "Money," he said. "Get a bottle. Fast." I was about to grab the boot when he snatched it back.

"No," he grunted. "No more drinkin'. I need food. Hell, Pound, I smell like a damn hog. I stink. I need a bath." He clutched his head in his hands. "Dear God, I'm gonna croak," he said. "Right here an' right now, I'm gonna die."

"You aren't going to die, Zeb," I said. "Give me some money and I'll . . ."

Stone peered into the boot. Then he stuck his hand in and moved it around. He stuffed a hand into his pants pocket. He was coming back to life rapidly, and he wasn't at all happy.

"Money? Give you some *money*? We spent forty

dollars last night and I ain't got a thing to show for it but pain!" Zeb lowered his voice, still cradling his head in his hands. "Look here, Pound," he said. "I owe you. I shouldn't have dropped you like I did. I was brung up better'n that. I . . . I feel bad about punchin' you, 'cause you ain't a bad guy. But I don't want no more booze. I'm goin' to eat something. You want to eat with me, well an' good. You eat with me. But I ain't drinkin' no more. Ever." He began to haul on his boot. I could tell that every bit of exertion—or even motion—must have felt like someone was taking a sledgehammer to his head.

"You comin'?" he asked.

Whiskey is better than food, but food is better than nothing. I didn't feel that I was in a position to negotiate.

"I'll eat with you, Zeb. Thanks."

Stone had gotten his boot on and was testing his legs to see if they could still carry weight. He wobbled and weaved a bit, but didn't do too badly. He hefted his saddle onto his shoulder, tottered slightly, but remained standing.

"Damn," he said. "First I'm goin' to buy me some clothes, then I'm goin' to get me a hot bath, a shave, an' a haircut. Then we'll eat."

We walked up the alley next to the blacksmith shop and out onto Main Street. Across from us, Tom Davis was just beginning to unlock the door to his mercantile. He looked at us but didn't say anything. His face looked like it would had he found a turd in his lunch pail. When he saw we were headed his way he shook his head in disgust.

"Don't bother coming any closer, Pound," he said. "I've told you you're not allowed in my store—and the same goes for your tosspot partner, too."

I stopped in the street. Zeb kept right on walking in that straight-backed, long-striding way of his. His boots thudded hollowly on the boards of the sidewalk as he approached Davis. He stopped a foot from the storekeeper.

"I want you to listen real close to me," Stone said, "'cause right now I don't feel too good. Sometimes when I don't feel good I get mean. You don't want that to happen. I been robbed. I had a good horse shot down and killed. I walked into this pissant town carryin' my saddle. I got drunk with Pound yesterday and last night. I *deserved* to get drunk." Stone stopped for a moment, spit on the sidewalk, and continued. "I need some clothes and I need a Colt revolver. I've got money. Now, the way I see it, we can do this in one of two ways. You can open your door and I'll come in and buy what I need. Or," Zeb nodded toward the large plate-glass window of the mercantile, "I can pick you up by your scrawny neck and throw you through the window, climb in after you, an' take what I want." Zeb nodded toward the glass again. "If I do have to toss you into the store, I'm goin' to pick up one of them cutter-plier tools you got there, an' I'm goin' to crunch the livin' daylights outta every tooth in your stupid head—one at a time."

A sheen of greasy sweat broke on Davis's forehead. It's a good thing for him that he already had his key in the door. His hands were shaking so badly, he'd never have gotten lock and key mated. He swung the door inward, jangling the big bell above it. Zeb stepped inside the mercantile and then stopped.

"Come on, Pound," he said. Tom Davis stepped aside as I walked into the store.

Zeb hurried up and down the aisles, grabbing what he needed: pants, shirt, summer long-johns, socks, and bandanna. Then he stopped at the glass-fronted Colt display case.

"Lemme see that .44 Army and the .45 single-action," he said. Davis near flew behind the case and banged the two weapons down on the wooden counter in front of Stone.

Stone balanced the .44 in his right hand, hefting it, handling it with sure, steady motions. He eased it into his holster and slid it back out. He did precisely the same thing three times. Then he dropped the pistol into its holster and let its own weight settle itself there. He made a tight fist of his right had, opened and spread his fingers, and then, almost instantaneously, the gun was in his hand. He grunted.

"Too heavy. Like tryin' to draw a anvil." Zeb dropped the .44 on the counter and tried the .45. He went through the same ritual he had with the first pistol. This time, however, he was smiling. His draw was a blur—too fast for my eyes to follow.

"I'll take this one," Stone said. "An' gimme five hundred rounds of ammo—Winchester, not that Army crap."

While Davis dumped boxes of bullets into a cloth bag and wrapped the clothing in brown paper, Zeb sat on the floor, dragged off his left boot, and brought out a pair of gold eagles. He was about to hand the money to Davis when he squinted at me.

"Damn, Pound," he said. "You look like a tall pile of buzzard droppings. You grab yourself some pants an' a shirt an' whatever else you need. An' get a hat. A man'll boil his brains an' go loco 'less he wears a hat in Texas in the summer."

I wasn't positive I'd understood Zeb. When he motioned impatiently and said, "Come on, Pound, I ain't goin' to waste the whole day in this pissant store," I started up and down the aisles at a handy pace. My clothes were little better than rags, and the only times they got washed was when I got rained on. I had no idea why Stone was outfitting me, but I wasn't going to question him about it. I picked up a chambray shirt, a pair of riveted denim pants, city underwear, as opposed to the long-john type cowhands preferred, a pair of socks, and a pearl-gray Stetson hat with a dark band. Stone pointed out that I'd been using a length of manilla rope as a belt and might just as well buy a leather one to keep my new drawers up. I did so. I also picked out a couple of handkerchiefs. It had been some time since I'd carried one.

Next, we crossed the street to Al Masters's barbershop. Early-morning traffic was moving in Burnt Rock, and Zeb and I got lots of quizzical looks and not a few snickers from the townspeople. Stone paid for a hot bath, shave, and haircut for us both. Slipping into hot water was a luxury I'd done without for a good long time. The sensation was wonderful. Zeb, in the second tub and separated from me by a cloth screen, groaned in ecstasy the same way a hound does when he scratches himself exactly where he itches. I could hear Zeb splashing about as he lathered up with the stiff brush and lump of soap Masters had provided to each of us. I followed suit. It was an embarrassment to see the amount of scum and dirt in the water before I was half finished. Unfortunately, bathing had not been a priority item since the town had dismissed me from teaching their youngsters. When I called Al and the two of us muscled the tub to the back door to dump it, the water looked like it had run off a dung heap after a heavy rain. As I settled into my second tubful, Zeb called out to Al to bring us each a cigar. Soaking in the hot water with a cigar clenched between my teeth and everything but my head submerged relaxed me so completely that I was more asleep than awake—kind of drifting along in my mind, at peace with the world. After a short time, however, a problem arose. My hands were beginning to tremble.

I needed a drink.

Stone and I dried ourselves with big, rough towels and dressed in our new clothing. When we left the barbershop, we reeked of bay rum and scented talcum powder, and I'd lost six inches or so of hair. My face was pleasantly warm and the slightest bit raw from Al's razor.

"Pound," Zeb observed, "you look like a new man. Your puss is as pink as a baby's bottom. How do you feel?"

"Different, Zeb," I said. "Different."

I thought—hoped—that Stone was headed for the

Drover. When he walked past the batwings and went into the restaurant next door, my craving for a drink was nudging me pretty hard. I felt an itching under the skin of my arms that had nothing to do with the layer of dirt I'd scrubbed off myself, and my mouth was dust-dry. My teeth began to chatter slightly, although the sun was already hot and the air humid. My fingers had the familiar lightness about them that indicated that they'd be quivering fairly violently rather soon. We sat at a table covered with a red and white checkered tablecloth, and Stone took it upon himself to order for both of us.

"Give us each a steak about the size of a saddle blanket," he instructed the waitress. "Cook 'em blood-rare and fry up a half-dozen aigs for each of us, while you're at it. An' . . ."

"Eggs," I said. "Not 'aigs.' The word is pronounced 'eggs.'"

Stone's deep-blue eyes focused on me for what seemed to me to be an uncomfortably long time.

"I always heard it aigs," he said. He turned back to the waitress. "An' bring along a big plate of fried potatoes and a pot of coffee, too."

I cleared my throat. "Zeb," I said, "I . . . uh . . . could sure use . . ."

Stone looked at the spastic little dance my hands were performing on the table and sighed. "I'd appreciate it if you'd send somebody next door to fetch a pint of the cheapest red-eye they can buy," he said to the waitress.

"A quart would—" I began.

"Nuts," Stone grunted. "Your lushin' ain't my

15

problem. Anyway, you got to quit bein' a bar rag sometime, don't you?"

I concentrated on my hands and didn't answer Zeb's question.

The pot of coffee and the pint arrived at the same time. I filled my cup three-quarters of the way with whiskey and added coffee to it. As usual, the whiskey worked its wonders almost immediately.

Watching and listening to Zeb Stone eat was an experience I've not matched before or since. He leaned far over his plate, elbows sticking out at right angles like the wings of a diving turkey buzzard, his fork in his right hand and his knife in his left, and began hacking large, ragged chunks out of the steak and stuffing them into his mouth. He'd chew twice or three times at the most, then swallow. There was a cadence—a rhythm—to his eating: hack, stuff, chew, swallow, hack, stuff, chew, swallow. The pace picked up when he attacked the eggs and the potatoes. I stared, fascinated.

Zeb must have sensed me gawking at him.

"Wassaproblem, Poun'?" he grunted around a mouthful of steak and potatoes the size of a man's fist. A yellow rivulet of egg yolk was running down his chin. "You never seen nobody eat before?" he asked.

"Not like that," I answered. "Not like that."

The meal in front of me was probably more food than I'd eaten in the last week. I was queasy at first, but after three cups of my highly boozed coffee, my appetite returned and I was suddenly ravenously hungry. I was doing the fine steak the waitress brought to me justice and was thoroughly enjoying it, when I noticed that I was no longer hearing slurping and snorting from Stone's side of the table. I looked up from my meal and found Zeb staring at me.

"I'll tell you this," he said, his tone almost one of awe, "you must be damned near starved, an' yet you cut off them tiny little pieces of beef an' dab them in your aigs jist so—all nice and slow—an' then you chew like a ol' cow workin' on her cud. You know what? You eat jist like a woman, Pound. Damn."

"If you equate eating like a civilized human being with womanhood, then I guess you're right, Zeb. But, as far as I'm concerned, manners are what separates humans from animals, and I elect to align myself with the former rather than the latter."

"Feisty today, now, ain't you?" Zeb observed, grinning widely. "Eat any ol' way you care to. It don't bother me none. I just kinda mentioned it to have somethin' to say, is all."

We stood on the sidewalk in front of the restaurant. Zeb patted his stomach and belched thunderously.

"Let's go in the saloon an' . . ." His eyes narrowed when he saw my smile. "Dammit, Pound," he snapped, "I ain't talking about drinking. What I want to do is get a sackful of dead soldiers and take us a walk outside town an' see if this new Colt of mine fires anywhere near straight."

I decided to await Zeb outside the Drover. Since he was so adamant about not having a drink—and not buying me one, which was the more important consideration—I didn't want to push through the batwings to watch others enjoying what I couldn't have.

As I stood on the sidewalk feeling pretty good about my spanking-new outfit, I noiced three of my former students come out of the alley next to the dress shop and begin to walk down the opposite side of the street. The two boys I recalled as being insufferably stupid and generally mean kids. They'd taken great delight, I remembered, in picking on a gentle young boy named Rodney, who'd apparently been born with less brainpower than his peers. They referred to him as Clodney, and took delight in sending the poor youth on foolish or impossible errands that always concluded with raucous, braying laughter at Rodney's expense. I was surprised to see Mary Nolan, a towheaded youngster of eleven, with the two boys. Mary had been a good student and a sweet young girl who had a decided talent in drawing and sketching. When they saw me, all three youngsters stopped and stared. The two boys put their heads together while eyeing me and I heard the semiwhispered words "drunk" and "boozehound." Mary, seeing that I'd heard the whispers, blushed prettily and stepped away from the boys, walking toward me.

"Mornin', Mr. Taylor," she said, standing in front of me. Her eyes were the blue of delft china and her almost startingly blond hair was pulled into two neat braids, one of which she worried between her fingers as she spoke to me.

"I'm sorry 'bout what them two are sayin', sir.

They're my cousins and I got to stay with them today. My ma's havin' another baby an' their ma is helpin' her out."

"I see," I said. "Don't let it worry you, Mary. I've heard worse. I hope your mother and the new baby are just fine."

Laughter sounded again from the boys and they no longer attempted to whisper their remarks. Mary blushed even more deeply.

"I . . . I thought you was a good teacher, Mr. Taylor," she said. "You never hit nobody like Mrs. Willis always done, and you helped me with my drawing. I . . . I wanted to tell you that. Lots of the other kids liked you, too. We didn't care if you was a drunk, Mr. Taylor."

I forced a smile for the child's benefit. "Thank you, Mary," I said. "I appreciate that. Now, you'd best go back to your cousins." She turned and hustled back to the two boys. I turned away from the street, peering into the Drover Inn. Zeb was standing at the bar. I could hear bits of conversation. The barkeeper was apparently running his mouth to Zeb about how Zeb was wearing both boots rather than carrying one today, but he shut up when Zeb said something too low for me to hear.

Zeb told him what he wanted. The barkeep scurried around quite a bit faster than I'd even seen him move. In a matter of a few moments, he handed a burlap sack full of empties to Stone, which he slung over his shoulder. Zeb tossed the bag of bullets to me and we started down Main Street. It was a hellaciously hot day to go for a walk. Every so often, I

took a pull at the quarter pint I had left from breakfast, trying to stretch it out by swishing the whiskey
in my mouth for several moments before swallowing.
On top of the big meal I'd just eaten, the cheap, raw-
tasting booze made bile rise searingly in my throat.
That didn't stop me from drinking it, however.

"This'll do," Zeb said after we'd trudged about a
mile beyond the end of Main Street. "You go out
thirty paces an' set them bottles in a line, 'bout a foot
apart from each other."

I dropped the bullets next to Zeb, took the burlap
sack, and did as I was told. I came back and sat on
the sand behind Stone—giving him plenty of
room—and had a suck at my very rapidly diminish-
ing supply of whiskey.

Stone fired six shots into the sand ten feet in front
of him as quickly as he could pull the trigger, then
rested the barrel of the pistol against his face.
"Damn," he said, grinning. "Nice an' cool. I don't
care for an iron that'll heat up."

He emptied the chambers of the Colt and reloaded
it. He did the draw my eyes couldn't follow, dropped
into a bent-kneed crouch, and blasted six shots at the
bottles. Nothing much seemed to happen to the targets. There was some splintered glass, but nothing
very dramatic.

"I think you're firing a tad high, Zeb," I said.

Stone spun and looked at me as if I'd just called
his grandmother a whore. "High? High?! I'm
shootin' at the very tops of the necks of them bottles,
and I didn't miss a single round. This here pistol can
talk, Pound." He was ejecting empty shell cases at

the same time he was hollering at me. "You want to see some glass busted?" he demanded.

"Broken, not bust—"

Stone wheeled back toward the bottles and exploded four of them with shots so rapid that the reports sounded like a single clap of thunder. He then shattered my pint bottle—which I was drinking from at the time—and, almost as an afterthought, blew my new hat off my head, putting a neat set of holes in the crown, which wasn't more than an inch or so above the top of my scalp.

"Lord," I said. "Lord."

"Come on, partner," Zeb said. "Give her a try."

"No, thanks," I said, picking up my hat. I poked a finger somewhat ruefully into the entrance hole and out the one where the bullet had exited. "I've never fired a pistol in my life. I'd just waste your ammunition. Perhaps another—"

"Perhaps nothin'," Stone said. "Come here."

I stepped up next to him. He handed me the fully loaded Colt, butt first.

"Now listen," Stone said. "Them bottles ain't goin' nowheres, an' they ain't gonna shoot back. You take your own sweet time an' bust them up good an' clean. Mind the kick, though. That thing ain't a peashooter."

My first shot was fifteen feet short, and the weapon jumped and twisted in my hand like an angry, living being. "Don't get to dependin' on that little sight," Stone instructed me. "It ain't worth a damn. Shoot her by the feel—you'll know when you're on target."

I put probably thirty bullets through the pistol without hitting anything but sand.

"Don't *think* about it, Pound—just *do* it," Zeb hollered.

Somehow, I shattered a bottle. It felt good. I'd begun to think of those bottles as enemies making me appear inept and foolish in front of Zeb. Then I shattered the one next to the first one I'd hit. I missed three shots and then took out another bottle in a highly satisfying explosion of glass.

"Whoooo—eeee!" Stone whooped. "Now you're gettin' the hang of it. Give 'em hell, Pound!"

I fired the Colt for another half hour. When I finished, I was sweaty and gritty and could barely hear anything other than a loud ringing in my ears. My eyes and nose burned from the pungent, acrid reek of gunpowder—and there wasn't a piece of glass in front of me larger than a double eagle. After I'd broken all the bottles, I'd shot at the pieces. There was something at work in my mind that kept me firing long after my targets were shattered. I guess fascination comes as close as I can describe it. I was standing there holding the power of life and death in my right hand. The largest, meanest, backwoods fighting man doesn't stand a chance against a puny ten-year-old with a pistol and enough strength to aim and pull a trigger. I'd heard that a Smith & Wesson beats a full house: Now I understood completely what was meant by those words.

Chapter Two

I hadn't realized it while I was shooting, but I needed a drink. My right wrist hurt and was swelling rapidly, and my arm and shoulder were beginning to throb with a deep, persistent ache. I had a blister on my forefinger from pulling the trigger. But even with my needing a drink, and considering all my aches and pains, I felt better than I had in a long time. It was rare that anything put drinking out of my mind for more than a quick moment. Even sex had no particular allure to me. But the combination of that Colt and Zeb Stone effected some sort of transient magic. Exactly why that was so, I have no idea.

Zeb must have noticed something about what I was experiencing just then. "You kinda like that Colt, Pound?" he asked. Actually, it was more of a statement than a question.

"I do," I said. "I do." I left it at that.

We trekked back into Burnt Rock and, without discussion, ended up sitting at a table in the Drover Inn. The stink of gunpowder still hung about me, in my clothes and hair. Zeb ordered a beer apiece and a pint of red-eye. He seemed suddenly tired, pensive, almost depressed.

"You're pleased with your pistol?" I asked.

"Yeah . . ."

"But?"

Stone sucked the foam off his beer, hesitated, and then spoke. "You know how many men I've killed and how much money I've made bein' a shootist?"

"No. I have no way of knowing such a thing." I poured an inch of whiskey into my beer. "I'm sure you're very good at it, Zeb. But such things are far beyond my—"

Stone interrupted me, but his voice was subdued and he spoke quietly, almost too low for me to hear. I had to lean forward toward him.

"Not a single man an' not a damned dollar. I've made all my money playin' poker. I wounded three fellas I was hired to kill. I could have taken all three of them betwixt their eyes—and I should have—but I put slugs in their arms an' shoulders an' such instead of killin' them. I gave the money back on each man. See, that's the point here: I didn't earn it. I was hired to gun them men an' I didn't kill them, so I didn't earn my pay. I was faster an' better than any of them, but I didn't kill them. In fact, I've never killed nobody at all."

I began to respond, but Zeb waved a hand, motioning at me to keep quiet. "I was supposed to kill, not pull feathers. Damn. Pound, as a shootist, I'm near as handy as a buffalo at a funeral. An' I been thinkin' on that. I had lots of time to think, walkin' all them miles."

I had no idea whre Stone was leading. "So?" I asked, but not sharply.

"So," Zeb announced in a louder, more confident voice, "I ain't gonna be a shootist no more. I ain't suited to it, an' I got to face up to that. I'm goin' into a different line of work."

"What will you do, Zeb?"

"I'll rob things: banks, trains, stagecoaches, stuff like that."

"Oh."

"Well, damn, Pound," Zeb said louder than he should have, "the James an' Younger brothers seem to be makin' a good living. An' there's lots of others doin' the same. Lookit Butch Cassidy, for instance. See what I mean?"

I was a little confused. "Why are you telling *me* all this, Zeb?" I asked.

He leaned toward me across the table. "Here's why: I want you to be my partner. A man alone can't rob nothin' much bigger'n a Sunday-school picnic. It takes at least two men to do a nice, solid robbery. I figure we can do good together, Pound. You ain't a full-fledged bar rag—'least not yet. Hell, man, we can get rich an' ride to Mexico an' live high an' happy 'til we curl up our toes of old age."

I drank deeply and avoided Zeb's eyes when I spoke. "I'm afraid you're talking to the wrong man," I said. "I'm no outlaw. I could never kill anyone."

"See, here's the thing: You don't *have* to kill

nobody—and neither do I. We'll do our robberies without hurtin' nobody. An' when we get rich enough—off to Mexico we go. See, Pound? I got her all figured out."

"But I've never stolen a thing in my life, Zeb. I don't think I could bring myself to do it."

Stone leaned forward in his chair. "You got a wife?" he asked.

"You know I don't."

"Kids or folks, then?"

"I haven't, but that's not the point."

"It *is* the point, dammit! What are you goin' to do the rest of your life? You sure ain't gonna be no teacher. Is scroungin' drinks an' sleepin' in alleys any way to live? Damn, Pound, you got nothin' to lose and a whole lot to gain. Does bein' nothin' but a drunk make you feel good? 'Course it don't. But you an' me, Pound, we can *be* somebody an' get rich an' retire."

"Zeb—I told you. I'm not an outlaw. You're talking to the wrong man. Maybe you've made some points. . . . Still—"

"Answer me this," Stone demanded. "What the hell do you have to lose? You answer that an' I'll leave you alone."

I poured the rest of the whiskey into my beer mug and swirled the mixture together before I drank. My mind was churning, tumbling, not focusing on any single thought. Of course, what Stone was proposing was patently ridiculous. I was neither a gunman nor a robber. Still . . . what *did* I have to lose—or, indeed, to look forward to?

26

Zeb went to the bar, returned with another pint of whiskey, and poured half of it into my mug. He sat back, sipping his beer, leaving me alone with thoughts. One memory kept repeating itself in my mind, making me cringe. I'd awakened one morning to find myself covered with horse manure and urine-soaked straw. Some of the kids who'd been my students found me passed out just about where Zeb and I had slept the night before, and they'd gotten shovels and covered me with a foot of dung from the stable.

I took a long drink of the warm beer/whiskey mixture in my mug. The entire concept Stone proposed was foolish. Men like Jesse James and Cole Younger and others of their ilk were born thieves and born killers—lovers of violence. In the course of my life, I'd never even been in a fistfight, much less pointed a weapon at anyone. And what I said to Zeb was true. I'd never taken a single thing that didn't belong to me. The picture of myself covered with manure kept flicking through my mind. It was obvious there was nothing in Burnt Rock beyond more drinking and more disgrace. But, even given that, there was absolutely no way I'd kill another human being.

I remembered how my already raggedy clothes had looked and smelled after I'd dug my way out from under the manure—and how the laughter of the men and boys on the street had sounded. I raised my mug and drained it.

Zeb shifted in his chair and cleared his throat.

"You must understand this, Zeb: I'll never kill anyone. Do you understand that and accept that completely?"

"Sure, Pound." Zeb stood and extended his right hand to me. "We got to shake on this to make her all official, an' then we'll be pards."

I pushed back my chair, stood, and took Zeb's hand. "Partners," I said. "Partners."

We did some more drinking in the Drover while I played with the idea of becoming a thief in my mind.

"You know, Zeb," I said, "we have a rather major problem."

"Nah," Stone answered cheerfully. "We'll get your snout outta the jug one way or another. Or at least we'll keep you sober when we're robbing—"

"I wasn't referring to my drinking," I said coldly, "which is my own business anyway. I'll carry my end of the load—you needn't worry about that. What I—"

Stone chuckled richly. "Needn't, huh? Damn. Who the hell ever says 'needn't'?"

I let that pass. "What I'm asking is how we're going to operate outside the law when we have no horses, I have no weapon, and we have no supplies of any kind?"

"Oh. Yeah. I see what you mean." Zeb slumped down in his chair. "Lemme think on that a little."

After perhaps three or four minutes had passed, Zeb sat bolt upright, the smile of a child at church beaming across his face. "I got it," he exclaimed. "We start right here in this pissant little town. We rent a couple of horses an' buy some supplies—jerky, coffee, canned stuff—tonight, an' then tomorrow first thing we rob the Burnt Rock bank. See?"

At first I thought Stone was attempting to be

funny, to make a big and stupid joke. Then I saw he was serious.

"That's idiotic, crazy. People here know us, or at least they know me. And the whole town has seen us together the last couple of days."

"So what?" Zeb asked.

"Damn it, Stone," I snapped, "they *know* us. They know our descriptions. They can identify us."

Zeb's face was serious and he spoke in a hushed tone. "It simply don't make no difference, Pound. We're gonna get knowed in a big hurry anyway. What's this town ever done for you 'cept boot you around like a stray dog? We got to start somewhere, pard. It might just as well be here as anywhere else. Seems to me you'd be real happy to step on some of the folks in Burnt Rock, after they fired you as a teacher and treated you so poor. Robbin' their bank's a good way to do it."

There was a certain absurd beauty to Stone's plan. He was quite right: The town hadn't done me any favors. The more I thought about robbing the Burnt Rock bank, the more I liked the concept.

"I suggest," I said, "that we each have a couple more drinks and that we then rent a pair of horses."

Zeb Stone was a good judge of riding stock. He picked out a pair of geldings, one a black and one a chestnut. He was to ride the black. We also rented a stock saddle, a pair of blankets, and a couple of low-ported bits in bridles. The stable owner insisted that Stone pay three days' rent on the horses and equipment in advance.

"I hope the ol' coot has lots of money in the bank," Stone mumbled to me.

We mounted and rode up and down Main Street a couple of times, getting the feel of the horses, before we stopped and tied up in front of the mercantile. I'm certainly no cowboy nor bronc-buster, but I've put some hours in on a horse's back. My chestnut seemed a solid enough animal, even if he was a livery horse. He had a smooth, comfortable walk, and I suspected his lope would be the same.

Zeb's funds were just about gone, and I certainly had nothing to contribute. Consequently, we bought only essentials: coffee, a quart of whiskey, several sacks of Bull Durham, a slab of salt pork, and two cans of cling peaches in heavy syrup. We sat outside the store while Stone hacked the tops off the cans with his Case knife. All of our other purchases were in a burlap bag tied to Stone's saddle horn. We ate our peaches and passed the whiskey bottle back and forth a few times.

Zeb looked around and behind us before he spoke. "How's the law in this town? I ain't seen a sheriff nor even a deputy since I come here."

"It's 'since I came here,' not 'since I come here.' The sherrif's name is Moe Morris. A more inept lawman doesn't exist. He's a known coward, too."

"What's inept?" Stone asked.

"It means . . . well—clumsy, stupid, unskilled."

"Oh," Stone said. "Good. How's this sound? We have our horses an' gear all ready tomorrow morning. As soon as the bank opens we walk in, I pull my iron, an' you snatch all the money and stuff it into

30

them cloth bags they have and we ride out headin' west. Before they get a posse together and mounted, we'll be long gone. Ain't that a nice, simple plan?"

I had to agree that it was.

We rode a couple of miles out of town and lazed the rest of the day away. At nightfall, we built a small fire from scrub and prairie grass. The evening was warm and clear, and the stars looked so large and close it seemed a man could almost reach up and touch one. Our horses were staked and I was at peace with the world, stretched out on my back with my head resting on the rented saddle. I had very little fear about robbing the bank, and absolutely no misgivings or second thoughts about the decision I'd made. In my mind, I was already an outlaw. Tomorrow would simply confirm that fact.

Stone hunkered down next to the fire. "Damn," he grunted.

"What's the problem?"

"A fat lotta good the coffee'll do us. We ain't got a pot, nor nothin' else to heat water in." He glanced over at me. "Any of that red-eye left?"

"A bit, Zeb," I said. "But make sure you leave enough for my morning bracer."

"Mornin' bracer, my foot," Stone said, but refused the bottle.

I slept amazingly well that night. I remember thinking as I dozed off that I'd never come across anyone so innocently criminal as Zeb Stone. To him, robbing banks and stagecoaches and so forth was simply a manner in which to make a living. It was as if he believed that some men chose to farm or to work in stores, and others chose to be outlaws, but that none of the pursuits were superior to any of the others. And I considered his comments about the poker game in which he'd won the horse: *I was playing a straight, honest game—hardly cheatin' at all.*

I decided one thing before I slept. Never again was anyone going to cover me with manure or laugh at me on the street. I wasn't the town drunk any longer—I was Zeb Stone's partner, and an outlaw, as well.

The early sun woke us. I immediately fumbled for the whiskey, my eyes grainy with sleep. I caught Zeb gawking at my trembling hands, and he turned away quickly, embarrassed. We saddled up and rode at a walk toward Burnt Rock with little conversation. Stone checked the load in his Colt and then spun the cylinder. It made a pleasant, well-oiled, whirring sound.

As we jogged down Main Street, we saw that there were three horses tied to the hitching rail in front of the bank. I looked over at Stone.

"No problem, Pound," he assured me. "Just some sodbusters scroungin' for a loan or somethin'. Don't go gittin' nervous on me. Everything's fine."

I looped our reins over the rail while Zeb untied the three horses and began shagging them away. He was about to slap a fine-looking bay mare on the rump to get her moving when his eye picked up the stock of the rifle in the saddle scabbard.

"Son of a bitch," Stone said in the same awed tone a preacher would use to say, "Thank You, Lord," over a miraculously healed member of his congregation. "It's *them!*" he bellowed. "That there is my Sharps—I

32

know from my initials in the stock!" Stone tossed the rifle to me and hollered, "Come on!"

I didn't like this at all. It wasn't part of the plan. A quick, cold sweat broke on my forehead. My thoughts ran impossibly rapidly. I saw Zeb and me with holes in our bodies, bleeding to death in the street. I saw myself in a cell. I wanted to swing onto my horse and make tracks out of town. *This wasn't part of the plan.*

We clattered across the sidewalk and burst through the doors into the bank. Two men stood with their backs to us, pistols leveled at four pasty-faced tellers. A huge, barrel-chested oaf faced us, bringing a rifle to his shoulder.

It was as if the entire scene were a tableau in a text-book. Motes of dust were suspended in the rays of sunshine streaming through the bank's windows. The backs of the two men holding the pistols were damp with sweat, and their shirts stuck to them. One of the tellers was holding a cloth sack in his hand, and another held wads of currency that he was about to stuff into the sack—but all movement, all action was at a dead stop. I could see the juice from a cud of chewing tobacco in the rifleman's mouth stop as it arced toward the floor. A double eagle was suspended between the counter and the floor, glinting in the sunlight. The barred windows in front of the tellers had not yet been shut for the day's business. One of the tellers was hugely fat, a pea of sweat was about to drop from his nose, and his face was waxy and ashen with fear.

The animal odor of the outlaws mixed with the

scent of the lilac toilet water one of the tellers wore. There was a tiny dab of shaving soap just under the right ear of the teller holding the sack.

It was so quiet in the bank that the creaking of the leather springs on a delivery wagon passing outside was loud enough to be frightening.

Then, from a state where all was stopped, everything was suddenly moving at a frantic, crazed pace.

Stone fired his Colt twice, shattering both knees of the giant holding the rifle. Blood spurted from each knee, and bits of whitish gristle exploded outward from the wounds. The robber screamed in a keening wail almost too high-pitched to hear and pitched over backward, flinging the rifle aside as he fell.

"Drop 'em or die!" Stone yelled at the other two thieves. The shorter of the men was in a crouch, spinning toward Zeb. Stone put two shots into the man's arm and shoulder, spraying a damp mist of blood into the air. The third man dropped his pistol—a Colt with bone grips—and raised his hands above his head. Stone stepped up to the man, picked the Colt up from the floor, and dropped it into his own holster. He then swung the still-smoking weapon he'd purchased the day before in a wide, powerful half-circle and slammed it into the outlaw's groin. Words do not exist to describe the pain in the sound the man made as he clutched at his privates and fell to the floor in a semifetal position, his eyes open so wide that they looked about to roll free from their sockets.

Main Street, which had been so quiet mere moments before, was suddenly thronged with running

34

and shouting men. Sheriff Morris, forehead dripping sweat and face an unhealthy hue of gray, sidled into the bank with a shotgun to his shoulder. When the tellers, all talking at once, filled Morris in on what had taken place, he strode back to the door and shouted to those outside:

"I've brought things under control in here. Somebody fetch Doc!"

The bank employees knew the sheriff had done nothing, and they didn't hesitate to tell anyone who would listen exactly what had transpired. Zeb Stone was suddenly a hero, and so was I—by osmosis or reflection, I suppose. I noticed I was still clutching the Sharps, but that I held it by the barrel rather than the stock. I couldn't have fired the rifle at all quickly if I'd wanted to.

We were just about carried down the street by the mob that had formed. We stood with our backs against the bar in the Drover Inn, and everyone there wanted to shake our hands and buy us a drink. This was fine with me. The fact that we'd intended to rob the bank rather than stop a robbery in progress mattered not a whit to either of us.

Zeb was lifting a schooner of beer to his mouth when he suddenly went pale, dropped his beer, and began crashing and shoving his way through the crowd. He barged through the batwings and flattened a cowhand who was just stepping in. Zeb took off at a full run for the sheriff's office, or, more exactly, for the hitching rail in front of Morris's office where the robber's horses were tied. Someone—we never learned who—had collected the mounts for the sheriff. Stone dug through the saddlebags of all three horses in much the same manner of a dog attempting to unearth a prairie dog. Miscellaneous junk from the bags flew in all directions. Stone found nothing: no cash and no arthritis bracelet. He stomped into the sheriff's office. After a very few moments, he stomped out again with a gunbelt and holster slung over his shoulder. He stood next to me at the bar once again. His face was a scarlet red and his hands were shaking. This time, men shoved *away* from Stone rather than to him. Zeb dropped the gunbelt on the bar and pulled the Colt he'd bought at the mercantile out of his waistband, where he'd stuck it after nearly gelding the outlaw with it. He dropped the pistol on the bar next to the holster and gunbelt.

"Put 'em on, Pound," he instructed. "It's all yours now. That lyin', no-good, backstabbin' lawman says he didn't find no cash nor no arthuritis bracelet on them men or in their saddlebags. Dammit, Pound, that's the second time that stuff has been stole from me! An' listen to this: We don't even get the horses! Morris says they got to be sold at public auction." Stone slammed his fist on the bar in anger and frustration. "We stop a damn bank robbery," he snarled, "an' we don't get a thing for riskin' our necks!"

"That's not true, my friend," said Edward P. Thurston, owner and president of the Burnt Rock Bank, as he let the batwings swing shut behind him. "I'm here to reward you personally." The crease in the bank owner's suit was razor sharp and his low boots gleamed with a high sheen.

"Well, that's damned sweet of you. Are you our fairy godmother or some such?" Stone asked sarcastically.

I nudged Stone sharply. "This is Mr. Thurston," I said. "It's his bank we saved from getting robbed."

"Damn," Stone mumbled. "This just ain't my day, Mr. Thurston. I didn't mean no . . ."

"No offense taken, son." Mr. Thurston's lips formed something close to but not quite a smile. He put his right hand to his vest pocket and removed a pair of ten-dollar gold pieces. He then handed one to Zeb and one to me.

Stone stared at his palm where the coin rested as if Mr. Thurston had dopped a steaming dog turd into his hand.

"Ten dollars?!" Stone bellowed. "We save your whole bank an' you give us ten dollars apiece? I ought to boot you through the roof of this dump, you scrawny little runt!"

Mr. Thurston backed away rapidly. When he was a few feet from the batwings, he stopped.

"I'm under no legal obligation to give either of you *anything*," he said. "There's no law that states I have to compensate a couple of swillpots for acting as any decent man would—and should. You're fortunate that I'm a generous man. Ten dollars is probably more money than either of you has seen in—"

When Stone pushed away from the bar, Mr. Thurston turned and ran. Just as he reached the swinging doors, Zeb's gold piece struck him squarely in the back with enough force to bring a yelp of pain from the banker. I walked over and picked up the coin.

Stone was smiling at me when I returned to his side at the bar. "You know, Pound, I have me a idea."

I returned the smile. "So have I, partner," I said. "So have I."

The next morning, the sky was the color of dirty cotton and there was a mist in the air that was far too cold for July. My horse had been anxious to get moving—to get his blood running to beat the clamminess of the weather—and he'd bucked a few times as Stone and I started down the road to Burnt Rock from the campsite we'd occupied the night before.

"Hang on to that boy, Pound!" Zeb shouted happily as the chestnut sunfished. "Show him who's boss!" I rode out the animal's high spirits easily enough and was pleased that Stone seemed impressed.

"You know your way 'round a horse, Pound. Damned if you don't. Where'd you learn to sit to a buck?"

"I was brought up around horses, Zeb. I began riding early and always enjoyed it."

"Your pa—was he a farmer or cattleman or some such?"

"Actually," I admitted, "he was a preacher with a very rich congregation. And our home was next door to a spread that raised short horses."

Stone built a pair of cigarettes as he walked our horses through the mist. His fingers moved with the sure and steady dexterity of a surgeon. My own fingers still had the early-morning tingles and were still trembling quite badly, although I'd drunk a half-pint of whiskey before we'd saddled up. Stone lit both cigarettes with a wooden match and handed one to me. It took me a few seconds to get my hand still enough to take the smoke from Zeb. If Stone noticed my problem—and he must have—he didn't say anything about it.

"You all clear on everything?" he asked. "You got it all straight in your mind?"

"Don't worry about me. I know what to do and I'll do it. You might look to your own duties instead of nagging at me. It's not like we're doing something terribly difficult."

"Damn." Stone grinned. "Bit snarly this mornin', ain't you, now?"

There were no horses at the rail in front of the bank this morning. We tied our horses and walked into the bank together. I pulled down the window shade, which said "Bank Closed" on it.

"Here we are again, folks," Zeb shouted. "Do what we say an' nobody'll get hurt!"

Two tellers at their windows laughed out loud—until Stone raised his Colt and thumbed back the hammer. "This ain't no joke," he growled. "Pound's coming through with saddlebags. All you got to do is load the money an' keep quiet." He nodded to me.

I stepped through the waist-high half-door to the teller's area and moved from one clerk to another, holding one saddlebag open. All four of them cooperated quite nicely.

My hands, I noticed, were as steady as they'd ever been. And I saw something in the tellers' eyes I hadn't seen in anyone's for some time—respect. Or perhaps it was fear, but the two are pretty much synonymous.

Edward Thurston stepped out of his office, a sheaf of papers in his hand. When he saw what was happening, he stopped, mouth gaping open, forgotten papers kiting to the floor.

"Damn nice seein' you again," Stone said. He waved toward Thuston's office with his pistol. "Everybody in the office an' down on the floor— now!" I moved along with the tellers and Thurston, tugging lengths of rope out of my second saddlebag.

"Tie our pal Thurston nice an' tight," Stone said. To the tellers, he said, "Ain't nothin' personal in this, but we got to tie the whole slew of you. Jist don't tense up nor fight Pound an' everything will be fine an' dandy."

I tied the bank president's hands behind him and then took several wraps around his legs, snugging the ropes and knots as tight as I could. I was a little less hard on the tellers.

Boots thudded on the sidewalk out front, paused for a long moment, and then thudded on.

"Come on, Pound. Gag 'em an' let's make tracks," Zeb urged. The strips we'd cut from our burlap sack the night before worked quite effectively as gags. As we were about to leave, Stone smiled down at Thurston.

"We figured on robbin' you yesterday, but them other yahoos beat us to it. Thing is, we added some little touches to our plan overnight—like the ropes an' gags. I guess I owe you for that, Mr. Thurston. Lemme pay you off like you done us." He dropped a ten-dollar gold piece in front of the banker. The tellers applauded with their eyes. We strolled out to our horses and rode off. Not a shot was fired. No one was hurt. Sheriff Morris was unable to mount a posse, and he was afraid to come after us alone.

Zeb Stone and I were officially on our way as partners and outlaws.

Chapter Three

Zeb and I had carried off a bit over four thousand dollars from the Burnt Rock Bank. It had seemed almost too easy, and I said just that to Stone.

"Beats hell out of shootin' men I don't want to kill," he answered. "Maybe every place we hit will be just as easy. But if they ain't, it don't really matter. I s'pose it's like any way of makin a honest living— some days is good, some bad."

I glanced at Zeb, expecting to see a big grin wrapped around the word "honest," but there wasn't one. I didn't see that I'd get anywhere questioning him on that point.

There was an element of surprise in the whole episode for me. The night before I'd wrestled a bit with the morality—or lack thereof—in what I was going to do. I'd never stolen as much as a piece of penny candy before, and I had what I believed to be a rational sense of right and wrong. Yet now, after the fact, I felt no regrets. Little Mary telling me that she and some of my students had liked me even though I was a drunk had something to do with how I felt. Certainly, I was a drunk—but beginning today, I'd be a drunk who takes what he wants rather than begging for it, a man who inspires if not respect in others, at least fear. I'd far rather be Zeb Stone's drunken partner than the stumbling town joke I'd become in Burnt Rock. I found it highly interesting that Zeb and I had roughly doubled a full year of teacher's pay with our first robbery—which took us a little less than ten minutes.

I'd been correct in my assessment of the abilities of the chestnut gelding. He had an easy, ground-covering, rocking-chair lope that was a pleasure to sit to and seemed natural and almost effortless to the horse.

We rode until it was too dark to see the ground in front of us and then pulled up for the night. Stone doubted that we were being followed, but decided against a fire. Neither of us was very hungry, and we had no coffeepot, so a fire wasn't anywhere near a necessity. We staked our horses and leaned back against our saddles. I was trying to roll a cigarette, and I was fumbling more tobacco around the shaking leaf of paper than I was getting on it.

Stone peered through the darkness at me, holding out his hand. "Here," he said, "lemme me do that. You're throwin' perfectly good tobacco all over the damned prairie." I didn't answer but handed over my makings. Zeb built a pair of smokes, lit them both with a wooden match, and handed one to me.

"You hurtin', Pound?" he asked.

"Yes. Badly." I'd gone equally long periods without a drink. I hadn't liked it then, and I didn't like it any better now. I felt as if I had ants all over me, and my nerves were vibrating like the strings on a well-played banjo. My throat kept on making swallowing motions, although there was nothing—not even saliva—in my mouth.

Zeb watched me closely for several minutes, then sighed and began pawing through his saddlebags. After rummaging around a bit, he handed a half-full pint of whiskey to me. I pulled the cork with my teeth and drained the whiskey in one long, life-giving suck.

"Pound," Zeb asked, still leaning toward me in the dark, "how long have you been lappin' up the booze?"

"I don't see how that is any of your busin—"

"It *is* my business. You're my pard. I got to be able to count on you, just like you got to count on me. I gotta admit that scares me some. Seems like there are three of us ridin' together: me, you, an' Mr. Red-Eye."

"Let me remind you, Stone, that you picked me as a partner. I didn't approach you. You knew then that I liked a drink."

Zeb snorted. "Liked a drink? Damn, Pound, you like a drink the way a fish likes water."

"Listen here," I began.

"No, you listen. I don't want to end up lookin' through cell bars for the rest of my life because you was too busy wantin' a drink to pay attention to what's goin' on. Maybe I didn't know how bad off you was. But listen—answer me this: Do you want to climb out of the jug?"

I hesitated. My shakes were gone, the ants were gone, and I rolled a cigarette that was as tight as any store-bought. "I've tried," I said. "Many times, I've tried."

Stone rose and began pacing back and forth in front of me in quick, nervous strides. "That ain't what I asked," he snapped. "I don't give a damn how many times you've tried. What I'm askin' is whether you want to beat booze or if you want to go on bein' a spittoon."

"Of course I'd like to beat it, Zeb. But, as I've said, I've tried and failed many times before."

Stone stopped his pacing and stared down at me. "There's this medicine that'll fix you up so you never want no more liquor, Pound. I know for sure that it works. A good friend of mine, he was a bar rag, just like you. Maybe worse, even. He took the medicine an' he straightened right out. He was a new man, Pound. A new man, an' a better one. All because of that medicine."

"How long ago was that?" I asked.

Zeb scratched his head. "Lessee—that was five—no, it was six years ago."

"Is your friend still cured?"

Stone hesitated. "Well . . . well, no he ain't. Fact is, he's dead. Damn fool passed out on the railroad tracks outside Dodge City and a locomotive haulin' a string of cattle cars done him in."

"Splendid," I said sarcastically. "If this medicine is so efficacious, why was your friend passed out on the railroad tracks?"

"What's efficacious?"

"It means helpful, able to aid."

Zeb chuckled. "'Efficacious.' Damn. There sure are lots of words I don't know. But here's the point, Pound: My friend had stopped takin' his medicine an' went on back to whiskey. If he'd kept takin' his medicine, he'd be alive today. We'll be hittin' a little burg called Morgansville tomorrow about noon. It ain't big, but they got a saloon and a general store. The store's pretty much sure to have that medicine. I disremember if Morgansville has a bank."

"There's no such word as disremember," I said.

"Sure there is. I heard it lots of times. Now, I figure we'll rest up for a few days in Morgansville and get you started on the medicine. You can guzzle a snootful tomorrow an' start the cure the next day. Does that suit you, Pound? Will you give it a try?"

"I suppose so," I said. "I suppose so."

We rode into the town quite a bit before noon the next day. I was pushing my horse harder than I should have been, and I knew that, but the craving was on me. Stone mumbled and cursed, but he kept up with me and didn't tell me to slow down.

Morgansville looked much like any of the shabby, false-fronted hamlets that are scattered throughout Texas. There was a plank sidewalk on one side of the dusty street, but not on the other. We saw little activity. A few horses were tied to hitching rails in front of the saloon and the mercantile—and, farther down, in front of the sheriff's office. An ugly, ribby, devious-looking yellow dog charged out to meet us, snarling and barking.

"Go on—git!" Stone yelled. I felt my horse tense

under me. Zeb's black crow-hopped a couple of times, eyes wide and rolling. The dog must have sensed the horse's fear and moved in closer, lips curled back and teeth bared. The black reared and danced, raising a cloud of gritty dust.

"Well, hell," Stone said. "I've had enough of this. Get a good hold on your horse, Pound." I did so. The dog rushed Zeb's horse again. Stone drew and fired twice. The slugs removed most of the dog's head. Zeb calmed his horse and grinned at me. "I never much cared for a mean dog," he said. "Damn—this Colt sure is effercacious, ain't it?"

Heads appeared at doorways and in windows. A lean, hatchet-faced man with a star pinned to his vest walked out of the saloon. We rode toward him.

"Get down from your horses," the sheriff said. I noticed the lawman's right hand, fingers very slightly curled, hung within an inch of the grips of the pistol in his holster. Zeb and I dismounted.

"Who plugged the hound?" the sheriff asked. His voice was deep and raspy, as if he had something wrong with his throat. It was then that I saw a livid, raised scar running across his neck from ear to ear.

"I did, Sheriff," Stone admitted. "The dumb sumbitch was rilin' my horse. A dog like that ain't worth the powder an' lead it took to blow him to hell."

The sheriff looked Zeb over very carefully.

"You wear that Colt low, son. You a gunfighter come to give me an' my town grief?"

"Nossir," Stone answered. "Me an' my partner, we just got paid off from a cattle drive and we're lookin' to drink some whiskey an' maybe play a little poker. Nothin' wrong with that, is there?"

"You're both cowpunchers?" the sheriff asked in that deep, somber voice.

"Yessir," Zeb said. I nodded in agreement.

"Horseshit. Neither of you is carryin' a rope or a bedroll. You ain't no more ranch hands than my grandmother is. I don't give a damn who you are, but I won't stand for no trouble in my town. Don't push me, boys, an' we'll get along fine. Drink your whiskey an' play your poker an' then ride on." He glared directly at Zeb. "And keep this in mind: I'm faster an' better than either or both of you because I *have* to be. Understand?"

We inclined our heads in agreement. "There'll be no trouble, sir," I said.

"You bet there won't be," the lawman growled. "There's a dollar fine for takin' the cur's head off. Pay up."

Zeb started to protest, but I quickly handed over a five-dollar bill. The sheriff folded the bill and tucked it into his vest pocket. "Remember what I said." He turned his back on us and began walking toward his office.

I looped my reins over the rail in front of the saloon and hurried inside. My armpits were flowing in torrents of nervous sweat, both from the craving for a drink and the chord of fear the raspy-voiced sheriff had sounded in me. I asked the barkeep for a quart of his best whiskey and two glasses. He was enough of a gentleman to pour my first drink for me, and he turned away as I did my best to get the glass to my mouth without splashing the contents all over the bar. By the time Stone joined me, I'd gotten down three inches from the bottle and was into the fourth and fifth inches.

Zeb leaned against the bar next to me and poured himself a drink. The few men who'd paid any attention to us soon turned back to their conversations, card games, and drinks.

"Morgansville's got a tin-can bank—'bout halfway down the block," Zeb said quietly.

"I thought you wanted to rest up—get supplies— start my cure," I protested. I'd been giving some thought to the medication Stone had described. I'd read medical science had made progress in many areas. It seemed to me that a significant percentage of men's problems had to do with the abuse of alcohol, and it only made sense that a medication to assist such men would be developed. "Let's give the medicine a chance to work," I suggested.

"I didn't say we had to rob the bank this minute, Pound. It ain't goin' nowhere. We'll rest, just like I said." He poured himself another drink. "I'm goin' to walk down to the store an' get us a coffeepot an' some peaches an' some of that medicine for you. This dump is a hotel. You stay put here. I'll get us a room. You hungry?"

"I suppose I could eat."

"Okay. I'll be back in fifteen or twenty minutes. Why don't you set at a table before you fall over. You like like you ate a dead rat." He looked more closely at me. "You ain't about to upchuck, are you, Pound?"

I drank half a glass of whiskey and weaved my

way to a table, glass in one hand, bottle in the other. "This whiskey," I said, "is without a doubt the worst rotgut I've ever tasted, and I've tasted them all. I hope the louse who owns this place has *all* his money—every last cent—in the bank down the street."

Zeb grinned and slapped me lightly on the back. "That's the way to think, partner!" he said happily. "Now you're catchin' on to this business, just like I knowed you would."

By the time Stone returned, I was quite deep in my cups. Two cowhands had joined me at my table and were treating me as if I were the brightest, most erudite being who ever trod God's green earth, primarily—and perhaps solely—because I was buying beer and booze as fast as we could drink it. Zeb strode to the table. He had a bulging burlap sack slung over his shoulder. I attempted to hand him a bottle. He shoved it away, disgusted.

"You two cow-flops get away from my partner," he said. The two men eyed Stone for a moment and then, in unison, pushed their chairs away from the table, stood, and lurched away, supporting each other.

Zeb sat down. "I got the medicine," he said. "I bought all they had—seventeen bottles. I got us a coffeepot, too. An' some canned meat an' peaches an' such. But here's what's most important." He reached into the sack and handed me a ten-ounce amber-colored bottle. I held it up to my eyes and squinted at the text on the label. I wasn't reading too clearly, and I had to go over the copy several times to get it all clear. It said:

DR. H. OLIVER'S POSITIVE CURE

FOR

ALCOHOL ADDICTION

This world renowned elixir is
prepared by Dr. H. Oliver in
his medical laboratory in
the city of Toledo, Ohio. It is
positively guaranteed to cure any
alcohol problem, regardless of its
severity, and regardless of the
length of its duration. Thousands
have been saved from lives of
degradation and intoxication by
this remedy. The afflicted
individual will notice great
improvement after only one dose.
The brain will be cleared of
toxic bile, the blood will be cleansed.
Bowels will become regular. The
user of Dr. Oliver's potion will
feel a delightful, healing sensation
of warmth and goodwill, and tremors
and foul stomach will disappear as if
by magic.
Take one generous dose when the desire

or need for spirits occurs. Continue
use until all symptoms of alcohol addiction
have been eliminated.

"See?" Stone asked excitedly. "Don't it say right there that you can bust the booze habit?"

"Break the habit," I said, "not bust it."

"Means the same thing both ways. Startin' tomorrow, you ain't gonna be a bar rag no more."

"Tomorrow?"

"Yep. I figure we'll take the bank in a couple of days an' get Morgansville behind us. That lawman is one hard-nosed ol' timber wolf, Pound. No two ways about that. So I figurt we'll get your cure working, rob us a bank, an' ride hard."

"But Zeb—I'm going to need at least some liquor to get me through this. I didn't start drinking yesterday. I've been at it for years—I'm *addicted* to it. I'll need—"

Stone cut me off. "Not a damned drop, startin' tomorrow. Only the medicine. You better load up tonight, Pound, 'cause there ain't no tomorrow for you when it comes to booze. I'll see to that."

I waved the empty quart to get the bartender's attention.

"Lord," I said. "Lord."

It was clear to me that Zeb had no understanding of how my alcohol habit had taken over my life. He thought I drank simply because I *liked* to. That, of course, wasn't the case. I drank because I *had* to. I planned to drink myself even beyond my standard stupor of intoxication that night, hoping that the effects of the alcohol would carry me long enough to find a way to get a drink without Stone knowing about it the next day.

The heat of the early-morning sun brought me slowly awake. I looked around as well as I was able without moving my head. The ceiling above me was spotted and stained, and pieces of scrap wood and newspaper were tacked up as patches. I was on a bed with a shuck-filled, sagging mattress. I reached under my pillow as segments—bits—of the day and the night before surfaced in my mind.

"It's gone, Pound," Stone said cheerfully. "I dumped the rest of your last bottle on the street after you passed out. Here—take a swig of Dr. Oliver's."

"Zeb, please . . ." I pleaded. "You have no way of knowing how I feel. I'm going to fly apart if I don't have a . . ."

Stone lifted my head with his left hand and held the amber bottle of medicine to my mouth with his right. He poured until I choked and coughed, gave me a few seconds, and poured again. A goodly amount of the medicine spilled down my chin and onto my chest, but I got quite a bit of it down. It was ungodly-tasting stuff with a thick syrupy sweetness to it, possibly to cover a sharply metallic flavor. Zeb lowered my head to the pillow. I dropped almost immediately into a deep, almost comatose sleep. I was dreaming about drifting far above the earth on the softest, whitest, most beautiful cloud that had ever existed, when Zeb shook my shoulder. I wanted to be angry with him for pulling me out of my dream, but couldn't.

"Pound," he said, "time for more medicine." I smiled up at him. We didn't spill any of that dose.

About nightfall, I sat up. The tingling, the ants, the tremors, the nausea, and the headache were all conspicuously absent. I felt genuinely good: mellow, relaxed, and hungry. Lord, I was hungry.

Zeb watched, fascinated, as I packed away two large steaks and eight fried eggs at the greasy little restaurant adjacent to the saloon. We were the only customers in the place, which was a fine indicator as to the quality of the food. That was all right: I was so ravenous that quantity was far more important than culinary excellence. I added a half-bottle of Dr. Oliver's potion to my last cup of coffee.

"You wantin' for a drink, Pound?" Zeb asked.

When I told him I wasn't, I was being totally honest.

Stone leaned close to me. I could smell beer on his breath and it bothered me not in the least. For the first time in a good many years, *I did not want a drink.*

"You done good, pard," Zeb said. That medicine is even better'n I thought. Now, the thing is, we gotta take that bank an' get the hell outta here. That sheriff scares hell out of me, an' it ain't often that I fear a man. He's always around. Every time I look up, seems like he's right there. Everywhere I go, he's there waitin' for me. He's near drove me nuts, an' we've only been here a day and a half."

Zeb looked at me as if he expected an answer. I nodded, sipping at my coffee.

"I figure it like this," he said. "I'll go to the lawman's office real early tomorrow mornin', draw down on him, an' lock him in one of his cells. He don't have no deputy. I learned that today while you was sleepin'. Anyway, you'll be at the bank with the horses. We'll charge in just like we done in Burnt Rock. The second time, I mean. We'll clean out the tellers an' make tracks. How's that sound to you?"

I nodded again. "Not only don't I *need* a drink, I don't even *want* one." Zeb stared at me for a long moment. He looked like he was going to ask me a question but decided against it.

"Let's go to our room," he said. "We got early work comin' tomorrow mornin'."

Chapter Four

I experienced the most vivid, most delightful dreams of my entire lifetime that night. I woke twice, took long pulls at the bottle of Dr. Oliver's I'd stashed under my pillow, and fell back into deep sleep almost immediately. I felt better than I'd ever felt drunk or sober—all without taking a drink. I came to the realization that I owed my life to Zeb Stone and Dr. Oliver, and I promised myself that I'd personally thank both of them for what they'd done for me. I further decided that I no longer bore even the tiniest iota of resentment or animosity toward the fine citizens of Burnt Rock.

The next morning, I looped our reins securely over the rail in front of the bank and waited for Zeb to jail the sheriff. Zeb assured me that the sheriff's cut throat and feeble voice would prevent him from making enough noise to fetch help to himself.

It was a fine morning. The sun was pleasantly warm without the driving force it would exhibit later in the day. I didn't, however, care to *blame* the sun for any discomfort it may cause with its oppressive heat—it was merely doing its job, and I commended it for its efforts. I drank a full bottle of medicine and tossed the empty onto the plank sidewalk. It made a pretty, bell-like sound as it hit. I wished Zeb were with me to hear that sound. The sunlight struck the bottle and created an almost painfully beautiful prism. I looked up and down Main Street to find someone to share that beauty with, but no one was out and about. The next thing I knew, Stone was shaking my shoulder.

"Come on, Pound! What the hell are you doing?"

His Colt was in his hand. I drew my own pistol and followed Zeb into the bank.

"This here's a robbery!" Stone shouted. "Raise your hands an' stay still an' nobody will get hurt. Move an' we'll blow your tails off!"

I stood behind my partner, smiling. "This is nothing personal, folks," I said. "You see, Zeb and I are going to live in Mexico when we rob enough—"

"Dammit, Pound!" Zeb hollered at me. "Get the money an' shut up!"

As I began placing money in a cloth sack, enjoying the fine texture of each individual banknote, we heard the rattle-thump of boots on the sidewalk, headed toward the bank in a big hurry.

"The sheriff got out somehow," Stone yelled. "Come on!" He fired a couple of shots above the tellers' heads and spun toward the door at a run. I followed, although not nearly as rapidly.

As Zeb collected his reins, I vaulted into my saddle. I hadn't mounted like that since I was a boy, but I did it quite competently.

Zeb's black dug in and started to run. I leaned forward and slammed my heels against my gelding's sides as Stone blasted past me. I heard shots. A slug whistled past my face. Another dug a shallow furrow across my horse's rump. My mount attempted to rear once, and then again. He squealed in fright and in pain, and again tried to rear. I banged my heels against his sides again, but he responded by squealing and shaking his head wildly.

Something was very wrong. Zeb had hauled his horse to a sliding stop and was galloping flat-out back to me, firing his Colt in the direction of the sheriff.

"Untie your damned horse!" Stone roared—just as the gelding tore the hitching rail free and began to buck in panic when the swinging five-foot-long rail slammed into his front legs and chest. A slug whizzed past my shoulder. The next one took my horse in the neck. A fountain of blood sprayed Zeb as he pulled his horse side by side with mine. I grabbed Zeb's shoulders and he spurred the black, pulling me onto his horse behind him. A bullet spun my hat away.

"That was my new hat," I said. The thought of losing it made me terribly sad.

"You stupid sonofabitch," Stone cursed, "hold on or I swear I'll dump you right here!"

The sheriff was eight or ten yards ahead, still on the sidewalk. We had no choice: We'd have to ride directly past him. His face was a crimson mask and his mouth was moving rapidly. I'm quite sure he wasn't praising the Winchester Arms Company. He was trying to feed another round into his 30.06, and the lever was obviously jammed. He was tugging and pulling and cursing, and, suddenly, he was moving the butt of the rifle to his shoulder.

"Use your gun!" Stone yelled. "I'm empty!"

I drew my pistol. We were five feet from the lawman when I threw the weapon at him with all the strength I could summon. Just as the butt of the rifle touched his shoulder, my pistol took him directly in the forehead. He dropped like a pole-axed steer. Zeb's horse's ears were laid back, and he was stretched out and running with all his heart. Stone kept on spurring, but a horse can run only so far at a full gallop, and that distance is shortened when the animal must carry double.

The black began to falter. The pounding cadence of the gallop was becoming sloppy and erratic. He was beginning to weave, and great, ropy strings of saliva were being torn from his gaping mouth by the rush of the wind. I thought that the animal had earned a rest, but when I said as much to Stone, he snarled at me.

At times in a man's life, something happens that makes him believe that there is a God or Spirit or whatever that watches over him and takes care of him.

This was one of those times. Riding toward us were two ranch hands. Their horses appeared stout and fresh. Stone slid the black to a stop and was out of the saddle and standing in front of the stunned cowboys, holding his empty Colt on them. The two men raised their hands high above their heads. I'd fallen off Stone's horse when he ground to a halt. I wasn't hurt.

"Get down, boys," Stone said. "There's no reason for anybody to get shot here."

Zeb unlaced his saddlebags and slung them over his shoulder.

"Mount up, Pound," he ordered. I chose the smaller of the two horses, an Appaloosa. I've always been partial to that breed. Zeb climbed onto the other, a strong-looking bay. Neither of the cowhands said a single word throughout the entire episode. I looked back at them as we sprinted off on their horses. They stood motionless, watching us. I waved to them. Neither returned my wave.

We put miles between us and Morgansville in what Zeb called the "Injun Way." This method of covering the most ground in the shortest possible time worked like this: We'd walk our animals for five minutes, lope them for ten, and gallop them for five, then repeat the same cycle over and over. Zeb estimated the times, as neither of us owned a watch. There was a mindless monotony to this type of riding that appealed to me. The Appaloosa I'd picked was a decent enough horse, and he carried me well. I'd put a bottle of Dr. Oliver's Positive Cure in each of the front pockets of my jeans, and I took a dose whenever I felt the need. The potion relaxed me and I had no desire whatsoever for alcohol.

I was so relaxed, in fact, that I fell off my horse several times in the course of the day. Stone would catch up with my mount, grab the reins, and lead him back to me, cursing and swearing every inch of the way. I'd dust myself off, climb into my saddle, and we'd set out again.

We traveled well into the night and stopped to rest our animals and get some sleep ourselves at about 2 or 3 A.M. We'd blundered onto a waterhole, although Stone insisted that he knew it was there and that he'd been heading for that very place all day. The water was tepid, brackish, and reeked of sulfur. That didn't stop us from drinking it, nor did it stop our horses. The buffalo grass wasn't high, but the grazing was adequate. We unsaddled and staked our mounts and settled ourselves a few feet from the water hole. I'd have liked to start a small fire so I could mix my medicine with coffee, but Stone wouldn't allow it.

Zeb had said very little to me since Morgansville, except to curse me when I fell off my horse, and to tell me he'd been riding to that water hole all day. I took a long dose of my cure.

"Why are you nettled, Zeb?" I asked. "We got away clean, didn't we?"

Stone exploded. "Nettled? Got away clean? Listen here, Pound: You damned near got us both killed. You screwed up a nice bank robbery. A good horse got done in 'cause you tried to ride him away without untyin' him from a hitchin' rail. You throwed away a perfectly good Colt revolver. You've been falling off your horse all day. You left the damned money in the bank. And you was as drunk as a buffalo hunter after a long, cold winter. You gave me your word, an' then you went an' got drunk." Stone was standing in front of me, his eyes locked with mine. His voice wasn't loud, but his intensity made the hairs on the back of my neck rise.

"*Drunk?* Zeb, listen—I . . ."

"I ain't done," Stone snarled. "I don't want no partner. I'll take my own chances. I'll be ridin' outta here in a few hours—alone. An' if you cross my path again, I'll put a hole in you big enough to drive a wagon through. It's a sorry, egg-suckin' hound who thinks more of his whiskey than he does of his pard."

Very slowly and very quietly, I said, "I didn't have a single drink, Zeb. Not one."

He snorted in disgust. "You was pickled, Pound. Don't lie to me no more."

"Not a single drink," I said. "Not a single drink."

Stone dragged me to my feet by the front of my shirt. His eyes were squinting, malevolent slits under the brim of his hat. I thought that he may kill me.

"Does a sober man do what you done?" he shouted, his face inches from mine. He shook me wildly, violently, the way in which I've seen a dog jerk and snap a snake, trying to chew through it and break it at the same time. Stone suddenly shoved me and let go of my shirt. I turned slightly as I fell, and I hit the ground hard. The bottle of cure in my right front pocket broke on the impact, and I felt a searing sensation as a jagged edge of the bottle cut through the denim of my pants and into my leg. I put my hand into my pocket and pulled out some of the glass. I held my fingers to my mouth and tasted the acrid, metallic bitterness of the medicine and the earthy saltiness of my blood. Then it hit me.

"The potion," I said. "The potion."

Stone stood in the pale moonlight, his fists clenching and unclenching almost spasmodically.

"The medicine, Zeb," I said. "I drank too much of the medicine. I was drunk on my cure!"

"Medicine don't make a man drunk, Pound. It . . . it just don't."

I thought I could hear the beginning of a doubt in Zeb's voice. "Drink a bottle," I said. "If you're so sure I'm lying to you, prove it."

"I ain't a drunk an' I don't need no Dr. Oliver's. It won't do nothin' at all to me, 'cause I don't need it. It would be like me drinkin' water, is all. The potion would just run right on through me, 'cause I ain't a drunk."

"Prove I'm lying," I said. "If I am, you'll know for sure you should ride off without me."

Zeb hesitated for a long time, standing perfectly still. Then he turned and walked to his saddle. I heard the muted clink of bottles ticking against one another. I unbuckled my belt and pushed my pants down to my knees and began picking shards of glass out of my leg. I took a good, long pull at the unbroken bottle of medicine from my left pocket.

It was twenty minutes—perhaps a half hour at the most—when Zeb came reeling over to me, taking a tentative step forward and then two quick steps backward, waving his arms for balance. He fell and hit the ground pretty much face-first. As he was pushing himself up, I could see that sand was sticking to the paths of tears down his cheeks.

"Pound," he said in a shaky, thick-tongued voice, "I done you real bad—worse'n I ever done anybody. I . . . I was ready to ride on out without my pard . . ." He made it to his feet and staggered toward me. "I'm sorry, Poun'. Can you shake my hand? I . . . damn, Poun', I . . ."

I stood and attempted a step toward Zeb, forgetting that I'd dropped my drawers. I fell just as Stone lurched forward. We slammed together, forehead to forehead. Both of us slept where we fell until the sun was well over the horizon.

At first I thought I was dreaming and that the chantlike sound I could barely hear was part of the dream. Then, as the fog in my mind began to dissipate, I realized that Stone was whispering to me, his murmur barely louder than a thought.

"Don't move, Pound. Don't move. Don't move, Pound. Whateverthehell you do, don't move."

I opened one eye. Zeb was on his side, his face pale under the layer of grit and dirt on his cheeks. His Colt was pointed directly at my head. The bore looked like that of a cannon.

I tried desperately to recall the words to a misty, vaguely remembered childhood prayer. I swallowed hard and closed the eye I'd opened, obeying Stone's litany. I wondered if the bottle of medicine he'd drunk the night before had warped his mind somehow. After all, I reasoned, he *wasn't* a drunk, and the potion was obviously prepared for those with severe booze problems. I swallowed again, but other than that I kept perfectly still.

The crash of the Colt's report was louder than I believed a sound could be. My head felt as if someone had split it open with a dull ax.

"Whoooo—eee!" Stone whooped. "I got that boy

nice an' clean! I'm goin' to make us hatbands out of his hide for sure!"

I pushed myself up and looked over my shoulder. A headless rattlesnake—the largest and longest one I'd ever seen—was writhing in its death throes. Blood was pumping out of the ragged, pinkish-gray stump that was left when Zeb's bullet had decapitated the creature. I leaned forward and vomited copiously.

Stone chuckled. "It ain't often you get to see a man with his drawers down pukin' his guts out."

I rolled away from the still-twitching snake and pulled my pants up. Stone replaced the spent cartridge and dropped his Colt into his holster. He was no longer chuckling.

"Them rattlers," he said, "they look around for anything warm when the air gets cool. You was it, Pound. He was right behind your head. I seen him soon as I woke up. I couldn't figure why I wasn't hearin' no buzzin' from him, but look there. He don't have no buttons." I looked at the dead snake. Zeb was right. Where the buttons should have been was a raw section of flesh and scales.

"Looks to me like somethin'—maybe a wolf or a coyote—had a tussle with him. Anyways, he kept bobbin' up an' down, an' I couldn't get a shot at him for a long time. But I put his lights out real sharp."

Stone's eyes shifted, avoiding mine. "You . . . uh . . . mad at me, Pound? You still want to ride together as partners an' all, don't you?"

I took a dose of medicine. "You didn't give me a chance to talk, Zeb. You even said you were going to ride on out without me, and you know I have no idea where we are. You wouldn't listen to me and you called me a liar. And remember this: The cure was *your* idea, not mine. It seems to me I'd be better off without you."

Zeb stared at the ground in front of him. "Yeah. Well. Damn. I already said I was sorry, Pound."

"That doesn't change a damned thing, Zeb! You tossed me around and treated me like a maggot, and I'm supposed to just forget it? Maybe my life in the jug wasn't much, but it sure beat riding with a lunatic who won't listen to his partner."

"I was mad, Pound. But didn't I come back for you at the bank? Didn't I catch your horse for you every time you fell off him yesterday? I was just mad at you, is all. I wouldn't have rode today without you. See, I ain't a doctor. How the hell was I supposed to know a man could get drunk on medicine? But look: We ain't got time to jaw. I don't know how far that lawman's territory runs, but I don't think it's real healthy for us to be in it." Zeb hesitated for a long moment. "You ridin' with me?"

I sighed. "I suppose so. I don't see that I have any options."

"You're ridin' as my pard, though, ain't you?"

"Yes," I said. "Yes. But I hope you learned something from all this."

Stone's eyes finally met mine. There seemed to be a little more glitter in his gaze than normal, but that may have been because he'd squinted so long waiting for a shot at the rattlesnake. As I looked at Zeb, the thought struck me that I hadn't had a real friend since I was a boy. I took Zeb's outstretched hand, and we shook. Then we saddled up and got the hell out of there. I had no more love for the sheriff of Morgansville than my partner did. Zeb forgot his rattlesnake.

We had more than four thousand dollars in Stone's saddlebags. Since we weren't more than a hundred miles or so from San Antonio, we decided to ride there, live it up for a week, tap a bank, and head, once again, west. We pushed our horses fairly hard, using the Indian method. We wanted to strike San Antonio at night. We planned to release the horses outside the town and walk in. News about stolen horses—and their descriptions—travels substantially faster than does news about a bank robbery. The average cowhand doesn't give a damn about banks, but a horse is very much a different matter. Many more than a few men have stretched ropes for being on the wrong horse at the wrong time or place.

Zeb commented, "Why dance on air for a bunch of gawkin' cowpokes when we can walk on into San Antonio and buy horses and gear with cash money—an' get legal bills of sale, to boot?" I couldn't fault my partner's logic.

I'd moderated my use of the potion. I'd take a couple of doses per hour, but not much beyond that. I had no desire for whiskey, and I stayed aboard my horse with no problems.

We ate the jerked beef and canned meat Zeb had purchased in Morgansville on the trail. We came upon shallow water holes often enough to keep our canteens full and our horses in decent condition. Late the next day, when the wagon and horseback traffic indicated we were closing in on San Antonio, we swung well away from the rutted wagon road we'd struck and followed, and set up a camp. Stone stripped the equipment from both horses and sent them on their way with slaps on their rumps. We built a small fire, made a pot of coffee, and ate canned peaches. I added a taste of the cure to my coffee every once and again.

The coals of the fire were dying, and the air was cool but not uncomfortable.

"You got big plans for San Antone?" Zeb asked.

"Not particularly," I answered. "A bath and a shave, a new Colt, a new hat, and as much beefsteak as I can eat will satisfy me. I need a supply of Dr. Oliver's. And a horse and tack, of course. What about you?"

Stone smiled and sighed. "I'm goin' to buy myself a new pair of boots. I'll play me some poker and drink some whiskey. An' I don't doubt I'll find me a pretty bar lady an' get my ashes hauled. Now listen up, Pound: Don't you go buyin' a horse 'less I'm with you. Some of them big-city horse traders will dump a plug with the heaves or croup or whateverthehell on a man who don't know horses real good."

"That's 'well,' not 'good.'"

"You know, Pound," Zeb responded, "one day somebody is goin' to boot your butt up between your shoulder blades on account of that schoolteacher talk you do."

"Perhaps," I said. "Perhaps."

"Perhaps nothin'," Stone said. "It's a damn fact.

Nobody had to correct none of my words before I ran into you. Folks understood me clear enough."

I emptied the last of a bottle of cure into my coffee. "That's not the point, Zeb. I'm sure you *were* understood. But what's involved here is simply a matter of right or wrong, correct or incorrect."

"How so?"

"Well—answer this: Could you put a saddle on a horse backwards?"

Stone pondered for a moment. "Sure," he said, "but it wouldn't fit worth a damn. See, the fork of your saddle fits over the withers—"

"Fine," I interrupted. "Then there is a right way and a wrong way to place a saddle on a horse. True?"

"Yeah."

"Well, it's just so with language, Zeb. There's the right way, and there's the wrong way."

Stone deliberated as he rolled a cigarette. He smoked it down to a nub and tossed it into the coals of the fire before he spoke.

"Nuts," he said. "Everybody I ever come across talks like me, but I never seen nobody ridin' a saddle on a horse backwards. Your argument don't make sense, Pound."

"Forget it," I said. "Forget it."

A couple of hours later, we each stuffed our pockets with money. What was left remained in Zeb's saddlebags, along with the few remaining bottles of the potion I hadn't gotten to. Zeb tossed the saddles, blankets, and the bits and bridles into the tall grass. "Mexican junk," he said, "held together with spit an' twine. Rich men like us, we don't ride no Mex saddles. I'll tell you this: I'm real partial to bein' rich. I'm gonna hit San Antone like a tornado—you see if I don't!"

We stumbled through the darkness to the wagon road and were fortunate enough to get a ride with a mule skinner who was delivering a load of lumber to San Antonio. Although the two large coal-oil lanterns that dangled from posts on either side of the driver's seat cast a good deal of light, the skinner seemed to have no interest in avoiding rocks, holes, or deep ruts. I asked him about this.

"Ain't my wagon," he said.

I pulled the cork on a bottle of cure and took a swallow.

"That ain't Dr. Oliver's, is it?"

"Yes it is," I answered. "I'm taking the liquor cure. And I'm doing quite well. I'd recommend Dr. Oliver's to anyone who suffers with an addiction to alcohol."

"Stuff is real effercacious 'lessen you start pourin' it down too heavy," Stone added.

The mule skinner shook his head in disgust. "You boys know what that slop is made outta? Tincture of opium, grain alcohol, an' water. Hell, I use it when one of my mares is birthin' an' havin' a tough time. Kills the pain. A doc, he told me about them patent medicines. He said a opium habit makes a booze habit look like a picnic in the park."

"I don't believe you," I said.

"Don't bother me one way or t'other," the skinner said. "I'm jist tellin' you what I know."

"But the label—" Zeb began.

"The label don't mean nothin'," the driver said heatedly. "Just because somebody wrote somethin' on a label don't make it true. That Dr. Oliver's stuff is poison an' it'll croak you faster'n booze will. It rots your brain an' such. Like I said, you do what you figure is right. I'm jist tellin' you what I know to be a fact."

I took a nervous swig of the cure. "This doctor," I asked, "what's his name? Does he practice in San Antonio?"

"John Holliday's his name. He's a tooth-yanker, not a regular doc. He ain't from 'round here. I met him in Dodge City." Me," the skinner went on, "I like a good, rip-snortin' three-day drunk as well as the next man. But I ain't got no trouble with booze."

We clattered and banged the rest of the way to San Antonio without much further conversation. Several times Zeb's and my eyes met, but we each looked immediately away without saying anything.

We entered the town from the north end of Main Street. Stone and I were rubbernecking like a pair of school kids on their first trip to a big city. And, in a sense, that's what we were. It had been several years since I'd seen anything but dusty cow and farm towns and saloon floors. Zeb had traveled, but he, too, had spent most of his time in insignificant little map-dots.

It was almost as bright as day on the street, and the tinkling of pianos and the shouts and laughter from the saloons washed over us like a wave of confused, frantic sound. The mule skinner jerked his rig to an abrupt halt. "Pile on out, boys," he said. "I pull down

71

the alley here to my freight agent's place." Zeb and I climbed down and nodded our thanks to the driver.

"Man's a idiot," Zeb said as the wagon pulled into the alley. "He don't know nothin' about Dr. Oliver's medicine. Hell, the only thing dumber'n a mule is a mule skinner, Pound. He's all wrong."

"I hope so," I said. "I truly hope so."

The Silver Slipper was the largest, most elaborate gin mill either of us had ever visited. There were twenty poker tables, and there was a large roulette wheel at the far end of the room. Lanterns were hung everywhere. A piano player with a stiffly waxed handlebar mustache was pounding away at "Buffalo Gals." There was a stairway leading to a balcony, and behind the balcony we could see a series of room doors.

"We got lucky, pard," Zeb said excitedly. "This place is a hotel, too. You reckon a beer'll do you any harm?"

I was about to accept Zeb's offer, given the fact that whiskey was my problem, not beer. But the point that there was alcohol in both beverages stopped me. As good as a beer would have tasted, I decided to let it alone.

"You go ahead," I told Zeb. "I'll just have a dose of my medicine."

We pushed our way through the crowd to the bar, Zeb carrying the saddlebags over his left shoulder. One of the three barkeeps looked our way and Zeb held up a single finger. The barkeep slid a schooner of beer to Stone. I put a dollar on the bar and Zeb hefted his mug. A huge bear of a man next to Zeb looked us over.

"You men new in town?" he asked. He was quite drunk. His eyes were as red as those of a mad dog, and his breath was rank enough to kill a rat in an open room.

"Just pulled in," Zeb answered with a grin. "We figure to take a room here for a few nights an' have us some fun."

The giant looked confused for a moment, then he spewed beer all over the bar in front of him in a raucous, donkeylike explosion of laughter. He elbowed the cowhand next to him. "These boys," he sputtered, "aim to take a room here for a few nights!" The second man broke into drunken, hiccuping guffaws. The back of Zeb's neck was reddening.

The bear shifted back to Stone. "You sodbusters ever been offa the farm before?" he bellowed, still choking with laughter. Zeb's neck was bright red, and the flush was spreading to his face. "This ain't no hotel, hayseed—it's a damn cathouse! Maybe you boys was lookin' for the church or somethin'!" Stone stepped back a bit from the bar. Here it comes, I thought, powerless to do anything. We hadn't been in town ten minutes.

"Zeb," I said. He ignored me.

"You asked us," Stone said, "if we've ever been off the farm. Now, lemme ask you a question: Was your ma a sow? I never seen a natural woman who could drop a hog like you."

The big man's hand reached for his pistol, and

then he stood perfectly still. There were two inches of Stone's Colt stuck up his right nostril. Zeb reached over with his left hand, lifted the pistol out of the man's holster, and handed it to me. At the same time, he jabbed upward with his own Colt. The giant was standing on the very tips of his toes. Blood was cascading down the barrel of Stone's weapon and was flowing onto both the floor and Zeb's wrist and arm. The men around us shoved and pushed at one another, getting out of the way.

"Now," Stone said, "I want you to do some singin' for me an' my partner. How 'bout 'Clementine'?"

"P-p-p . . . p-please," the big man stuttered. His voice was high-pitched, reedy, comical in a man his size.

"Clementine," Stone said, pushing another half-inch of gun barrel into the bear's nostril.

"Ohh . . . mmy darlin' . . ." the giant began in the little-girl voice.

"You sing real good," Stone said. He twisted his Colt sharply. The cracking of cartilage was muffled but audible. Zeb withdrew his pistol and shook it, spraying blood around him.

"You keep outta our way," Stone commanded. "An' if you got any ideas about gettin' some of your litter mates together an' comin' after us, remember this: You go down first, an' you go down dead."

I pulled Zeb toward the batwings. The gamblers, shopkeepers, and cowpunchers parted to let us through. I dragged Zeb outside and hurried him down the block.

"Zeb," I said, "you've got to calm down a bit. You

can't go sticking your pistol in people's noses just because they josh you a bit."

Stone wiped the barrel of his Colt carefully on the leg of his denim pants, spun the cylinder to make sure it moved freely, and dropped the weapon into his holster. "Sure I can, Pound," he said affably. "Matter of fact, I just did."

Chapter Five

We stopped in front of the longest series of plate-glass windows either of us had ever seen. There were five sections, each measuring about eight feet in length and six feet in height. Centered and painted in black, gilt-edged script were the words "Scott's Mercantile." Although the store was closed, there was enough light from the lanterns on poles along Main Street to allow us to see at least the front displays.

"Lookit all them saddles!" Zeb exclaimed. "I bet there ain't a single piece of Mex leather in any of them! An' lookit all them rifles. I goin' to buy me a Winchester tomorrow. An' you can pick up . . . Wait in minute . . . you don't need no pistol, now, do you? Lemme have a look at that iron."

The pistol Zeb had handed me in the Silver Slipper was riding comfortably in my holster. I drew it and handed it to him.

"Damn," he said. "You got real lucky. This here's a Smith and Wesson .44. They make a good revolver, Smith an' Wesson does. Now, I like a Colt myself, but that don't mean nothin'. An' a .44's got a good bit of punch, Pound. No reason for you to buy an iron now, is there?"

I sighed. "No," I said. "But the way I got this—"

"Come on, Pound," Stone interrupted. "We're partners, ain't we? You don't have to thank me for the pistol."

We took a room at a place called the Harrison House. Stone stashed the saddlebags under one of the beds. We locked the door and set out to find a restaurant. That didn't take long: There must have been a dozen eateries on Main Street. We selected a spot called Anne's simply because it was close and wasn't crowded. I poured half a bottle of cure into my first cup of coffee. At soon as we were served, we began packing away beefsteak and fried potatoes like a pair of hungry hounds set free in a butcher shop. It was approaching midnight when we finished eating.

"Ready for some sleep?" I asked.

"Sleep? Hell no! I'm goin' to find me a poker game!"

"Zeb . . ."

"Don't worry, Pound. I'll play straight and won't prod nobody. I'll tell you this, though: Even without cheatin', I play a better game of poker than anyone I've ever come across. See, it's in their eyes. I can tell in a second when somebody's bluffin' me. Same thing on raisin', too. I just watch their eyes, an' I know when to back off an' when to bet a bundle. Plain fact of the matter is I can't be beat at poker." He handed me one of the keys to our room. "See you later, pard," he said.

Paul Bagdon

I smoked a cigar as I strolled back to the Harrison House. There were a few newspapers in the shabby lobby of our hotel, and I sat in an overstuffed chair and looked over the papers. I opened a copy of the *San Antonio Courier* and my eye was caught by a headline on the second page:

DRUNKEN DESPERADOES ATTEMPT MORGANSVILLE BANK ROBBERY!

Two men, both of whom were described as intoxicated by employees of the Morgansville Bank and Land Company, fumbled an attempt to rob that institution. One of the would-be thieves endeavored to ride his horse away from the scene without first untying the animal from the hitching rail. Sheriff Will Gates was slightly injured in the course of a gunfight with the desperadoes. Thanks to the Sheriff's heroism, the bank sustained no loss. Law authorities hypothesize that the perpetrators of the Morgansville incident were the same two outlaws who robbed the Burnt Rock Bank, making off with over four thousand dollars.

I read the story twice and decided not to mention it to Zeb. The newspaper writer had made us out to be a pair of buffoons. Stone wouldn't like that. Neither did I.

I went up the stairs to our room, undressed, had a swallow of Dr. Oliver's Potion, and fell asleep almost as soon as I stretched out on the lumpy and sagging mattress. Several hours later, Stone stumbled in drunk, mumbling, and cursing about "them no-good, cheatin', underhanded riverboat gamblers." I went back to sleep.

Zeb shook me awake the next morning. "Come on, Pound," he said, "get on your feet. I want to do our buyin' an' get the hell outta San Antone. An' you can forget about the bank. There's a damned sight more soldiers in this town than there are regular folks. An' I'll tell you this: The poker here is as crooked as a backwoods lawyer."

"How bad?" I asked.

"I . . . uhh . . . 'bout a thousand or so. All I had with me."

I pulled the cork from a bottle of Dr. Oliver's and took a sizable swallow. There were things I wanted to say to Zeb, but it was evident he wasn't in the mood for conversation.

We paid for our room and walked down a block to the barbershop. From there we went to Scott's Mercantile. We bought made-in-Texas saddles, bridles, bits, and blankets. I picked out a fine Stetson and a pair of saddlebags. I bought twenty bottles of medicine, wrapped each in newspaper, and put them in the saddlebags. Stone hefted and dry-fired a dozen or so rifles before he selected a Winchester lever-action .44-40. We bought jerky, canned condensed milk, coffee, Bull Durham enough to carry us to Armageddon, canned peaches, ammunition for all our weapons, and a pair of oilskin rain slickers. Zeb looked over the boot display, shaking his head in disgust.

"I wouldn't trade the boots I'm wearin' for anything you got here," he growled at the clerk. "Where can a man get himself a decent pair o' kicks?"

"You've got to have them custom made," the clerk said.

"How long's that take?"

The clerk scratched his chin. "Well, maybe a few weeks, a month—I don't know."

"Damn," Stone said. "I could be dead by then."

I didn't like the way that sounded.

We lugged our purchases down Main Street to the livery stable and horses-for-sale operation. Stone rode nine horses before he selected a muscular, solidly built roan gelding for himself. He rode seven more and then picked a tall black gelding for me. Much to the amazement—and delight—of the stable owner, Stone paid the asking price. We got solid, signed-and-dated bills of sale that described each horse to the most minute detail of coloration, scars, and the like. We saddled up, the new leather creaking and complaining as we pulled our cinches and attached our gear. Zeb wrapped his Winchester in his rain slicker and tied it behind the cantle of his saddle.

We mounted our new horses and rode to the restaurant we'd patronized the night before. I opened a fresh bottle of potion. Stone was strangely and uncharacteristically quiet through breakfast—at least in terms of conversation. His hack, stuff, chew, and swallow routine was, as usual, accompanied by enough slurping and grunting to put a pig to shame.

I figured that if Zeb had a problem he wanted to discuss with me, he'd do so.

I didn't have much of a wait. Stone swirled the dregs of coffee in his mug.

"These cities," he said, "San Antone an' such, are no damned good for me an' you, Pound."

"Why?"

" 'Cause they're too damned big, too noisy, an' just too damned many people around. An' too much law. There are more badges on the street than a man can shake a stick at. It—all of it—makes me jumpy. You know?"

"Yes," I said. "Yes."

"There's a little place called Dry Well 'bout sixty, seventy miles or so due east. It's our kinda town."

"Oh? Why?"

" 'Cause we're low on cash," Zeb said. "See, Dry Well has a nice little tin-can bank. I seen it last year, comin' through this way."

"Fine," I said. "Fine."

"You know," Zeb said, "you're near drivin' me crazy with your repeatin' words all the time like you do."

I nodded without speaking. We paid for our meals and walked out to the hitching rail. Stone hesitated before mounting, grinning at me. "Don't let it bother you none, Pound," he reassured me. " 'Bout the words, I mean. Lots of folks are screwy in one way or another."

We began the ride to Dry Well.

After some initial bickering, our two horses

seemed to accept walking side by side with each other. I was pleased with the fluid smoothness of my black's gaits. Zeb felt good about his roan, as well. Both horses appeared to have been excellent choices. So, although our mounts gave us no problems, there were at least a couple of other complications. One was the weather. The heat in August in Texas is far more than a reading on a Sears and Roebuck thermometer. The sun saps the life and the energy from all living things. I'd heard that good men—family men and churchgoers—would stumble back to their homes after a half-day in their fields and beat hell out of their wives or children for no apparent reason. Solid and trusted dogs and horses turned mean. Partners and best friends beat one another senseless with their fists over inconsequential disputes that would barely merit mention in less feverish times.

Paradoxically, the heat worked in my favor, leading me to a decision I may well not have made had I not been addled by the sun.

The comments of the mule skinner who'd given us the ride into San Antonio repeated almost nonstop in my mind. That Dr. Oliver's Potion could be dangerous was a given. My actions in Dry Well certainly established that. I couldn't help but wonder if I was merely exchanging one addiction for another. The potion affected me much as whiskey did, and I was drinking it as I had whiskey, keeping at least a mild state of intoxication going at all times, and hitting the bottle heavier when I wanted to go to sleep. When I'd been late with my morning dose, I'd felt the ants again and seen the trembling in my hands.

That I was addicted to Dr. Oliver's was fairly evident. I'd purchased twenty bottles in San Antonio, when three or four should have sufficed. That was precisely the manner in which I'd bought whiskey when I had the money to do so—buying and hiding bottles so I'd never be caught without.

I continued to think as Stone and I continued to ride through what felt very much like hell. We pushed our horses no faster than a walk, and even then their chests and sides dripped, and their tongues lolled from the sides of their mouths. I hadn't known a man could sweat as I did. I was as wringing wet as I would have been had I stood in a driving rainstorm for an hour. My thoughts churned and swirled, and tiny red and black spots danced before my eyes. Great sheets of shimmering heat appeared ahead of us like gigantic translucent windows that distorted the horizon and the flatly arid landscape. That first day of the ride to Dry Well disgusted me within myself: My perspiration—my entire sweat-soaked body—reeked of Dr. Oliver's Positive Cure for Alcohol Addiction. Stone wouldn't ride next to me. He spurred his horse a couple of strides ahead of me. He said he couldn't share the same air with me. I couldn't blame him. I was foul, disgusting, malodorous. And, like a tune or a song I couldn't put out of my mind, the skinner's words echoed over and over: ". . . tincture of opium, alcohol, and water . . ."

I sipped at one of the amber bottles and could feel bile rise in my gut to meet the tepid medicine I was drinking.

"Zeb?"

"Yeah?"

"This ride will take what—three days?"

"At least four, Pound, and maybe five. We'd kill our horses movin' any faster. We ain't gonna do nothin' but walk unless the weather changes. An' I'll tell you this: The weather ain't gonna change."

I fit the cork back into the bottle and made my decision, acting on it before I had a chance to change my mind.

"Stone!" I called, lofting the bottle high out and in front of my partner. He drew and blasted the bottle out of the air. I threw five more bottles as fast as I could unwrap them from the newspaper. Zeb didn't miss a shot. I gave him time to reload and pitched six more bottles in front of him. Again, he didn't miss. Zeb replaced the spent cartridges in his Colt, but dropped it into his holster.

"I ain't shootin' no more," he said.

"Why not? I've got more bottles . . ."

Zeb turned in his saddle. His face was running wet, but his grin was wide and strong—and proud. " 'Cause the rest of them sonsabitches are yours, pard."

We reined in and dismounted. Stone carried the remaining bottles of cure out about twenty feet from me and walked back.

"Give 'em hell, Pound," he said.

I did. The Smith & Wesson acted almost on its own, its barrel swinging to and spitting lead at the bottles. I ran perhaps fifty rounds through my pistol, reloading as fast as my shaking hands would allow.

When I finished, there was nothing left but shattered amber glass, an acrid, hazy-blue cloud of gun smoke, and a heavy, medicinal fetor in the air. I turned to Zeb. He'd been holding the horses about ten feet behind me. We mounted and rode on. Zeb matched the pace of my black with his roan, shoulder to shoulder with me.

To say that the next four days were hell would parallel stating that the War Between the States was a disagreement. But when I rode down the Main Street of Dry Well, I was a full, unbranded, unowned man. I wasn't stupid enough to think I could beat the type of habit I'd been carrying for so long in a few days. But I had a handle on it—and a good, strong handle, at that. I was shaky, but I was keeping food down and I was no longer experiencing the irrational, panicky swings of emotion that had been plaguing me for the first three days. I was having trouble sleeping at night, but I figured that would take care of itself. After all, I'd pretty much forgotten how to fall asleep naturally. I'd relied on the sleep-inducing qualities of alcohol for several years, and then I'd switched to opium, an even more potent relaxant.

Dry Well was a quiet, torpid little town. There were apparently enough successful ranchers and farmers in the area to support a general store, a boardinghouse and restaurant, a saloon, a combination barber/undertaker, a stable, a lawman, and, of course, a bank. Zeb swung straight for the saloon, but I rode down the block to the general store. I wanted *all* new clothing, boots and hat included. Everything I'd been wearing, including my Stetson, was permeated with the now stomach-turning stink of Dr. Oliver's elixir. I bought everything I needed and then spent almost two hours soaking in very hot water, alternately relaxing and scrubbing myself with a rough brush and a lump of soap. Finally, powdered, bay-rummed, clean shaven, scoured pink, and newly outfitted, I joined Zeb at the saloon. I handed Stone one of the cigars I'd bought. I caught myself staring at the bottles behind the bar and quickly looked away. I still *wanted* whiskey very badly. But, it seemed to me, I now had a choice in the matter, and that choice hadn't been available to me for several years.

When the barkeep set another schooner of beer in front of Zeb and moved away, Stone nodded toward a hefty, baldheaded fellow who was slumped forward on a table, his arms cradling his head. He was asleep—or passed out—and was snoring as loudly as only a drunk can snore.

"That fella," Stone said, "is the sheriff. He's the only law in the whole damned town."

"Well," I said. "Well."

I was sucking happily on my cheroot when two cowhands, laughing loudly and obviously already foolishly drunk, burst through the batwing doors. They bellied up to the bar a few feet from us. The larger of the two men made an exaggerated show of tilting his head back and sniffing noisily.

"I'll be damned," he said to his friend. "I smell me a French whore, right here in Dry Well!"

I looked at Zeb. He looked back at me. "All yours,"

he said, " 'less his pard sticks his nose in where it don't belong."

I've never been a fistfighter and I never will be. And the situation certainly wasn't one that called for gunplay. Still, the cowboy was shooting his mouth off at me for no good reason. I made what I felt to be the most auspicious move, given the circumstances. I stepped away from the bar, stooped down and picked up a wooden chair by its rear legs, and smashed it over the cowboy's head. He went down like a puppet whose strings have been cut. The dry wood of the chair split and splintered. The barkeep reached for something behind the bar—probably a shotgun—but I was faster. I dropped a gold eagle on the bar.

"I had a little accident and damaged one of your chairs," I said. "Will this cover your inconvenience and the replacement of the chair?"

The barkeep scurried down and grabbed the coin. "I reckon it will, an' it'll buy your pard another beer, an' anythin' you want, too."

The remaining cowpuncher was doubled over, laughing and gasping at the prone figure of his friend. "Les," the bartender said to him, "you lug that knucklehead outta here and don't neither of you come back 'til you're sober."

Zeb placed a dollar on the bar. "No harm done," he said. "A cowpuncher ain't worth a damn 'less he goes off on a toot once in a while. Give them boys a drink. Me an' my pard was just headin' out, any-how." We left and walked across the dusty street to the boardinghouse and restaurant. Zeb stopped me at the door to the restaurant. "Damn," he said, shaking his head, pride glinting in his eyes, "you sure do take to this outlawin', Pound."

The sheriff had slept through the whole episode.

After three full days of rest and good food for us and for our horses, we decided to take on the Dry Well Trust Company. The hot weather had been broken by rain, but Zeb and I were both getting fidgety, so we decided to hit the bank regardless of the downpour. We'd been wet before, we decided, and we'd be wet again.

Zeb went through the door to the bank first, with me a step behind him. I turned the Open sign in the window of the door to the Closed side, and pulled down the roller shade. Zeb drew his Colt and stepped to the center of the room. "This here's a stickup, folks," he announced. "Nobody needs to get hurt. Just do what me an' my partner say, an' everything will be fine."

There was a long moment of shocked silence. Three tellers and a tall, cadaverously thin man in a fine-looking suit were huddled together at a teller cage. A fourth teller was at his cage. In front of him, on our side of the cages, was a white-haired old gent with a beard that reached to his waist. Standing next to him was a grandmother-type old lady whose back and shoulders were hunched forward a bit, as if from the weight of all the years she carried.

The man in the suit stepped forward, away from the three tellers. "See here . . ." he began.

"Shut your yap an' keep it shut," Zeb snarled at

him. "I got no love for bank owners, an' that's what you look like to me. It's up to you: Run your mouth and I'll shoot holes in you. Shut up an' you live. Which is it?"

The man stopped midstride, turned in a tight half-circle, and went back to stand with the tellers, his face pale, his mouth tightly shut.

Zeb nodded to me. I vaulted over the counter and moved from cage to cage, stuffing banknotes into a cloth bag I'd picked up at the first cage.

"Young man," the old lady called to Stone. Her voice was strong, but there was a slight quiver in it. It struck me that she was more concerned than afraid. As it turned out, I was right.

"Is it banks you rob, or do you steal from hard-working farm couples, as well?" she asked.

"Ma'am?" Zeb responded, unsure of what he'd heard.

"I asked," she said, "if you were going to steal our money, or just that of the bank."

Stone kept his eyes—and his Colt—on the three clerks and the tall man, knowing that I had control of the fourth clerk and the old folks.

"We don't rob nothin' but banks an' such, ma'am," Zeb said. "Your money is safe from us."

"Not until Mr. Dodson here completes our receipt, our money isn't safe from you," she said.

I'd stopped to listen to the exchange.

"Move it, Pound," Zeb ordered. "We don't want to spend the whole damned day here."

"You'll not use profanity again in my presence," the lady said, her cornflower-blue eyes flashing. "I've

taken a switch to bigger and better men than you!" I
noticed the quiver was gone from her voice.

"What I'm saying is this," she went on as if she
were addressing a thickheaded child, "if Mr. Dodson
writes our receipt, our money here belongs to the
bank. If he doesn't, it's still ours, and the bank
doesn't have to pay us back."

Zeb smiled broadly. "You—Dodson," he said.
"Finish up that receipt for these folks." The teller
bent over the piece of paper in front of him. As he
wrote, I cleaned out the cash in his drawer and then
swung back over the counter to join Zeb. The teller
blotted the receipt and passed it with a trembling
hand to the old lady. Her husband, who appeared to
be even older than the woman, watched the entire
exchange without saying a word. For all I knew, he
could have been a mute.

"Is it all done up right an' proper?" Zeb asked.

The lady inspected the paper. "It is," she answered. "We thank you boys."

The elderly fellow finally spoke, his voice deep
and powerful for such an old gent. His smile was
wide and completely toothless. "We're buying a piano from Sears an' Roebuck in Chicago," he said.
"Victoria here plays right well." He pronounced the
word "pie-ano."

After we'd herded all of them into an office, I tied
and gagged everyone securely—except for the old
couple. I merely looped lengths of rope around their
wrists and ankles and I left their cloth gags loose. I
wouldn't have done even what I did, but I feared the
law might question why the old folks weren't tied.

The rain had eased off while we were in the bank, but the day remained dark. Not a trigger was pulled in the robbery, and we cleared slightly over three thousand dollars—all of it the bank's money. Since we'd seen the sheriff nowhere but the saloon for the past few days, I assumed that's where he was during the robbery. Or perhaps he was home in bed at that early hour. Either way, it made no difference. Zeb had been correct. Robbing banks was easy.

We rode well into the night. When we halted, Stone was sure we weren't being followed. There was enough scrub and mesquite to build a small fire, even though it was still wet from the earlier rain. The two of us leaned back against our saddles, smoking cigars and drinking Old Government Brand Fine Coffee.

"Well, pard," Zeb said, "you done right good. You upped an' beat hell outta whiskey an' Doc Oliver, all in one crack. An' that ain't sayin' nothin' about that cowpuncher in the saloon."

I held my right hand, fingers extended, closer to the light cast by the coals of our campfire. The tremor was obvious. "I want a drink so badly right now, I'd probably kill for a bottle," I said. "I haven't beaten it, Zeb, and I doubt that I ever will. But I'll tell you this—I'm not going back to it. I'll lose these shakes eventually, and my stomach will get back into better order, too. But don't you tell me I've beaten anything, because I haven't. At best, I've fought it to a draw."

Zeb was quiet for a few minutes, thinking. "You're better off than you was, though, ain't you?"

"Much," I said. "Much."

91

"See?" Stone said, dismissing the subject. "Look—I've got me a idea. We've done three—well, two, anyway—banks. What we're gonna do now is rob us a stagecoach."

"Where?"

"I've been thinkin' on that. Our best bet is to hit one headin' into San Antone, but way the hell out. We don't want to be nowheres near the town. See, the incomin' stages almost always have a cash box on board. Hell, it'll be easier than a bank."

I considered Zeb's proposal. "Don't the coaches carrying money have an armed man riding with the driver?"

"Sure," Stone answered. "An' the driver'll be carryin' iron, too. But that ain't a problem, as long as we got the drop on them. Them men ain't goin' to risk their lives for no stagecoach company. The drivers an' shotgunners don't make enough money to keep 'em in beer an' cigars. No man in his right mind would trade lead with a pair of outlaws for the money they're paid."

"Fine," I said. "But how do we get the advantage on the driver and the guard?"

"Easy." Stone grinned. "I got her all figured out. First, we swing back to maybe twenty miles outside San Antone. All the stages use that road we was on. When we see one comin', you hang sideways in your saddle like you was dead or hurt real bad. I'll drag a leg like I was wounded an' I'll cover my Colt with a bandanna an' I'll wave the coach down. They'll figure we was took by outlaws. When the driver reins in, I'll pull the bandanna off my iron an' you come alive, along with your two friends."

"Two friends? What . . . ?"

Zeb howled with laughter and slapped his knee. "Your best friends outside of me, pard—Mr. Smith an' Mr. Wesson!"

I failed to see much humor in the situation. I still wasn't completely comfortable with the idea—or the reality—of carrying a weapon. Nevertheless, Zeb's plan seemed basically sound. "What about the passengers?" I asked. "Are they likely to be armed?"

"Naw. Women an' easterners, pard, that's all they are. If some drummer or gamblin' man is carryin' a hideout Derringer or some such, he ain't gonna pull it. See, we don't rob the passengers, anyway. They stay right inside the stage, nice an' quiet, while we get the cash box an' the driver's an' shotgunner's guns an' make tracks."

I didn't respond. We were quiet for what seemed to be a long time. Somewhere off to the south we heard the yipping of a coyote and, a few moments later, an answering howl from then north.

"Pound?"

"Yes?"

"You sleepin'?"

I sighed. "How the hell could I be sleeping if I answered you?"

"Yeah. Well. Anyways, how much money do you think we got to steal before we cross the border? To live high an' fat for the rest of our lives, I mean."

"I've given that some thought. I suggest we go

over when we have twenty-five thousand dollars apiece."

Zeb whistled long and low. "That's one fine bundle of money. I guess you know what you're talkin' about, though. We got lots of years left to live. An' even if we went busted in Mexico, we could always cross back an' steal some more, right?"

That irritated me. It wasn't part of the plan. "No," I said. "This isn't a game we're playing. What we're doing can put us in prison for the rest of our lives. Think about that. Once I set foot in Mexico, I'm not coming back—ever. And if you have the brains of a buffalo, you'll do exactly the same. I've had enough conversation. Let's get some sleep."

"Feisty tonight, ain't you?" Stone laughed quietly. "Damn if you ain't became a real outlaw, Pound."

I ignored Zeb. Eventually, what little life was left in the coals of our fire expired. A single, hopeless-looking tendril of pale smoke drifted upward and was gone. A short time after the fire died, I slept. We made the ride back to San Antonio in three days.

We'd watched the approach of the stagecoach, or, rather, the plume of dust it raised, for the last hour. Although the clouds had begrudgingly set free a few sprinkles of rain, the temperature was rising. The heat was steamy, humid, difficult to breathe.

Stone checked the load in his Colt, untied the large red and white bandanna from around his neck, and draped the sweaty-damp cloth over the weapon, concealing it.

"Time to get to the road, Pound," he said. I noticed

a tightness in his voice that seemed to be born not of fear but of anticipation.

I put my left boot into my stirrup, half mounted, and then leaned forward, hanging over my saddle. My pistol dug into my abdomen where it was pressed between me and the leather. My arms and hands hung limply, convincingly, on the right side of my horse. Zeb led both of our mounts to the middle of the furrowed, beaten path of a road. When the stagecoach was within clear sight, he pulled his horse ahead a few strides and began waving the bandanna frantically.

"Here they come," he said.

I could hear the pounding of hooves and the creaking of the leather sling-springs and dry wood of the coach body. The cadence of the hoofbeats slowed. Stone was barely within the vision of my left eye. He was leaning against his horse as if for balance and support, his right boot held a foot or so off the ground. The coach horses broke to a walk, snorting and sucking air. The driver pulled the brake and stood, looking down at Zeb. The passenger compartment was ten feet or so away from me, on my right. The man riding next to the driver rose also, a shotgun in his left hand.

"What's going on here?" the driver demanded. "You hurt, son? What's . . . ?"

"Yessir." There was pain in Zeb's voice. "We been robbed. They gunned my brother. They killed . . ."

The guard dropped his weapon on the seat and began to climb down from the stage. "Let's see how bad you're . . ."

Stone pulled the bandanna from his Colt, pushed away from his horse, and stood on both feet.

"Mornin', gents," he said. "This here's a stickup. Toss the cash box down an' keep your hands way the hell away from your guns. We ain't out to draw no blood unless we have to."

I clutched my pistol in my right hand and slid down the left side of my horse. I couldn't see into the passenger compartment through the grime- and dirt-encrusted blinds.

"You passengers stay right where you are and don't make a move," I said, surprised at how level and strong my voice sounded. I heard a gasp from within the coach. "Stay where you are and you won't get hurt. This doesn't concern you folks. We're not . . ."

The barrel of a rifle poked out from under the forward blind, leveled directly at Stone's chest. The angle was all wrong: Stone couldn't possibly see what was happening unless he turned his head, and he was concentrating on the driver and the guard. Without conscious thought, I raised my pistol and fired twice into the passenger compartment. For an eternity, everything was completely still, and the reverberating reports of my pistol were the only sounds in the universe. Then there came a hideous, horrendous, screaming wail from inside the coach.

A toy rifle fell to the ground, putting a puff of dust into the air. The coach door swung outward and a blond young woman in a gingham dress was framed in the opening, her face a contorted mask of horror and shock. She cradled the body of a small boy—

perhaps five or six years old—in her arms. The back of the boy's head was missing and blood was pumping from a ragged, gaping hole where his throat should have been. I stood stunned, unbelieving.

The guard dove for his shotgun and the driver's hand flashed toward his pistol. Stone's Colt barked twice. The woman was screaming again—or maybe she hadn't stopped. I don't know. I couldn't move. My mouth was framing words on its own. I was saying over and over, "I'm sorry. I'm sorry."

Stone backhanded me—hard. "Come on, Pound," he hollered. He was already next to his horse, swinging into his saddle. I mounted woodenly, my eyes still locked on the woman and her child. Stone grabbed my reins and buried his spurs in his horse's flanks. We galloped away from the road, out onto the prairie. The scream followed us. My pistol was still in my hand. I dropped it into my holster. Zeb pulled to a stop and handed my reins to me. Our eyes met.

"It was a boy with a toy rifle," I said.

"Let's ride," Stone said. There were tears on his face.

Chapter Six

We urged our horses until mere urging had no effect. Then we prodded—forced—them forward with spurs and boot heels, and finally, with cruel, stinging cuts with our reins on the sides of their necks. We stopped only when our path cut water, and then for the briefest possible time. It was as if we could somehow diminish the horror, the sheer, cold-blooded evil of what we had done by putting miles between us and the stagecoach and the child's body.

Stone's horse began to stagger before mine did. They'd both been dragging the toes of their hooves for the past couple of hours, stumbling and lunging forward to keep from dropping. The wet, croupy whistle of their breathing told us that the animals didn't have far to go until we literally killed them with our lunatic pace. Zeb reined in and dismounted.

"We can't go no farther 'less we travel on foot," he said. "These two ain't gonna make another quarter mile. We'd best give them what water we have and rest them for a few hours."

Stone jerked his cinch free and stripped the saddle and blanket from his horse. I did the same, and saw that my saddle blanket was dripping wet, as if it had been completely submerged in water. I'd never treated a horse that way before.

Zeb and I each took a mouthful of water from the two canteens apiece we were carrying and dumped the rest in our hats for the horses. Stone had bought two pairs of hobbles in Dry Well. As we secured the hobbles, neither horse had enough energy left to resist. "They're too beat to go anywhere," Zeb said, "but we can't take no chances."

We leaned back against our saddles and listened to the halfhearted attempts of our mounts to graze the sparse scrub. Their respiration was hoarse and uneven. An hour—perhaps a bit longer—passed. Zeb sat up and rolled a cigarette.

"Pound?"

"Yes?"

"Everything—the whole shootin' match—is different now. You know that, don't you? Ain't nothin' the same."

"I know," I said.

Stone went on as if I hadn't spoken. "See, in some of them towns like Burnt Rock an' Dry Well, some of them yahoos might have come after us for a bit, but I doubt it. Nobody much gives a damn about a bank robbery. If the truth be knowed, most folks are kinda happy to see a bank get took. It maybe makes up for how the bank screwed them in one way or another. Know what I mean?"

"A murdered child is something else, though, isn't it, Zeb?"

"Yeah, it sure as hell is somethin' else. A posse don't bring no kid-killers back alive. It's like a man who puts out a lawman's lights. He's got about as much chance of seein' a jail an' jury as a block of ice has in hell. People don't want to catch us no more, Pound. They want to kill us. Real bad, they want to kill us."

Zeb took a final drag of his smoke and flipped the nub out into the darkness.

"You know somethin'?" he said. "We're dead right now—we just ain't been buried yet. Folks who ain't got nothin' will dig through their pockets an' come up with a dollar or five dollars to put toward bringin' in a hired gun to get us if the law can't do it. I'm faster an' better than most of them, but I ain't faster an' better than *all* of them. An' remember this: The shootist gets his money whether he faces us both one at a time in a fair fight or if he blows holes in the backs of our shirts from a half mile away with a Sharps on a damn tripod, loaded for buffalo." He sighed. "We're dead, pard."

My voice caught in my throat. "I didn't know it was a toy! I thought—"

"Don't matter what you was thinkin'. The thing is, a little kid's dead. An' you pulled the trigger on him. Or *we* did. One's just as guilty as the other in somethin' like this. You know all that guff you hear about law in the West? Far as I can see, all that pretty much comes down to three things: You don't steal a man's horse, you don't mess with his woman, an' you don't kill his kid. Hell, I know you was just coverin' me. I ain't blamin' you for nothin', Pound. I know I killed that shotgunner. I took him right in his heart. I more'n likely killed the driver, too. We're in the kinda trouble nobody gets out of."

I didn't want to think, to talk. If there were decisions to be made, I wanted Stone to make them. "What do we do now?" I asked.

Zeb drew his Colt and replaced the two rounds he'd fired that morning. He spun the cylinder and it made that clicking-whirring sound.

"Hole in the Wall is too damned far," he said. "We'd never make it. I figure we head for Houston. That lady seen our faces real good, but she ain't gonna remember what we was ridin'. If we haven't wore out the two we have, we can keep the same horses. We ride hard to Houston an' come into her from opposite ends. We split the money we have an' we buy new clothes—dude stuff. We don't carry no guns an' we keep away from each other. We can meet at a bar called—lemme think—O'Neill's, that it. Yeah. O'Neill's. It's on Main, near the courthouse. We put our horses in different stables. There's at least three in Houston. We stay in different hotels. When we meet at the bar, it'll be kinda accidental-like. It'll be just a pair of fellas jawin' about nothin', like everybody does in a saloon. We grow beards an' get our hair cut different. If we make the ride to Houston, we might have a chance. It's the only shot we got. Unless you got a better plan, that's what we'll do. We ain't in a position to be picky."

I hadn't realized I'd been crying until Zeb stopped speaking. Then I felt the tears on my face and the aching tautness in my throat. "I put two bullets into a child, Zeb. I killed him."

"I know. We can't do nothin' to change that. All we can do is ride to Houston or give up. Is that what you want to do—give up?"

I shook my head. I was numb, but at the same time, I was scared. "How long do you think it'll be before they're after us, gunning for us?"

"Hard to say," Zeb answered. "The lady an' the kid was the only passengers, right?"

"I don't . . . I didn't see any others."

Stone rolled another cigarette, deep in thought. "Well, we got to figure someone come on that mess back there within a couple hours or so. They'd have to ride to San Antone for the law, an' the sheriff would have to scratch up, supply, an' mount a posse. 'Course, they wouldn't damn near kill their horses the way we done. If the lawman knows what he's doin', he'll circle the stage in wider an' wider circles 'til he picks up our tracks. We shouldn't be ridin' together, but we are. Thing is, it kinda points us out nice an' clear. Anyways, I'd say we got maybe a five- or six-hour lead. Maybe a bit more if we're lucky, an' a bit less if we ain't."

"But if we make Houston, we can more or less lose ourselves in the city until it's safe to ride on, correct?"

Zeb spat off to his side. "You ain't been listenin', Pound. We're *never* gonna be safe again. Never. There'll always be a gun behind us or waitin' for us."

"But . . ."

"No buts an' no maybes, Pound. I know what I'm talkin' about."

I nodded, no longer trusting my voice.

"The sheriff from San Antone will lose our tracks way the hell outside of Houston," Zeb said. "It's a big place, an' there's lots of traffic goin' in and comin' out. He'll go to the law in Houston with our descriptions. But hell, Pound, we look like everybody else. There's nothin' too special about us. An' we'll be duded up an' not spendin' much time together. If we don't get killed on the way, we got a chance to pull this off. It ain't a big chance, but it's better than no chance at all."

I thought over all Zeb had said. It seemed to me that in a wild, bustling, growing, bursting-at-the-seams place such as I'd heard Houston to be, a couple of separate strangers who didn't stir up any attention wouldn't have any more impact than a pebble tossed into an ocean.

"Zeb," I said.

There was no response. I listened closely and heard Stone's even, slightly sibilant breathing. He was asleep.

Each time I closed my eyes, the image of the woman's face and the horrible spewing of blood from the hole in the boy's throat forced me to open them again. I went back over what had happened, recalling every sound, every sensation, every thought I'd had. There was no way in the world I could have known that the barrel pointing at Zeb was a wooden one connected to a toy rifle. I told myself any sane man would have done what I did—and immediately recognized how insane, how totally self-serving that thought was. I asked myself what I'd become and couldn't find an answer, a definition. I'd taken a young life. At one time, I'd taught young boys; today, I'd killed one. And for what? A few hundred—or a few thousand—dollars? We'd left the cash where it was, and neither of us had mentioned it in the course of the day or night.

I wanted a drink more than I'd ever wanted one before. I *needed* the safe harbor booze had always provided. If I'd had a bottle, I'd have drunk it without giving a thought to my hard-earned sobriety. But I didn't have a bottle. I'd have settled for Dr. Oliver's potion, but I didn't have that either. All I had was myself and my thoughts and memories of the morning.

I eased my pistol from my holster. The metal was cool—almost cold. The weapon seemed heavier than it had in the past. And it seemed infinitely more evil. I thumbed back the hammer and heard it click into place. I recalled how my two shots had sounded almost a day ago. I put the muzzle to my face. The residual smell of gunpowder made me wrinkle my nose involuntarily. The hard rubber grips of the Smith & Wesson held the pistol tightly to my palm, even though both my hands were suddenly leaking sweat.

I put the barrel to my right temple, feeling the hardness of the metal against my hair, my flesh. My index finger rested lightly against the trigger. All it would take was a bit of pressure.

My hand began to tremble, and the weight of the pistol pulled itself downward, to my neck. I moved the barrel to touch my throat where my bullet had struck the child. My finger curled inward slightly, moving the trigger a hairsbreadth toward the point of no return.

After a long, long moment, I brought my weapon down, eased the hammer back to safe, and put the pistol into my holster. It was a basic and rather uncomplicated decision: I preferred to go out as an outlaw rather than as a suicide.

Stone prodded me awake at the very first hint of the melancholy light of false dawn. I sat up, rubbing my eyes. I hadn't dreamed of the woman or the child. Although the incident had taken place less than a full day ago, it had already begun to fade, to become slightly diffuse at the edges in my mind. My revulsion at what I'd done hadn't actually lessened. Rather, it was being pushed into the recesses of my consciousness by a more powerful, more urgent emotion: fear. I was afraid to be caught. I didn't want to be shot to pieces and left for the carrion eaters by a posse. What was done, was done. Neither my death nor Zeb Stone's would change that fact an iota. My muscles were stiff and ached dully, and my mouth was dry and tasted foul, coppery, like bad water. I stood and stretched, trying to loosen the painful tautness of my neck and shoulders. Stone moved from horse to horse, pressing his ear just behind the shoulder of each on both sides. His eyes were closed tightly and he was straining to hear.

"We sure didn't do these two no good yesterday,"

he said, "but I don't hear no rattles or wheezes. I doubt we busted their wind. They'll carry us to Houston."

I hefted my saddle and blanket and moved toward my horse. Awkwardly, he turned his rump to me and attempted to move away.

"Damned good thing I bought them hobbles," Zeb said. "If they was only staked, they'd bust in our heads before we could get our gear on either one. Make sure your saddle is set good an' you got a tight hand on your reins before you slip the hobbles. These boys see a repeat of yesterday comin' up, an' they don't like it a bit."

I had to clear my throat a few times before I could speak. "How far is Houston?" I asked.

"Couple hundred miles or so, due north an' east."

"How long will it take us?"

Stone pulled his cinch and slid his hand between the saddle blanket and his horse's back, searching for wrinkles that could rub holes in the roan's hide. Festering saddle sores can make a horse just as use-less as bad hooves can.

"Three days an' part of a night," Zeb answered. "If we don't do in that, the posse will be close enough behind us so's we can reach back and shake hands with them."

"Can we make it?" I did my best to keep my apprehension—my fear—out of my voice. "Will the horses hold out?"

Stone swung into his saddle. "I dunno, Pound. But we ain't gonna get a chance to find out if we stand here jawin' all day." I slipped the hobbles, keeping a

GET
4 FREE BOOKS!

You can have the best Westerns delivered to your door for less than what you'd pay in a bookstore or online. Sign up for one of our book clubs today, and we'll send you **4 FREE* BOOKS**, worth $23.96, just for trying it out...**with no obligation to buy, ever!**

Authors include classic writers such as
LOUIS L'AMOUR, MAX BRAND, ZANE GREY
and more; PLUS new authors such as
COTTON SMITH, TIM CHAMPLIN, JOHNNY D. BOGGS
and others.

As a book club member you also receive the following special benefits:
- **30% OFF** all orders through our website & telecenter!
- **Exclusive access to** special discounts!
- **Convenient** home delivery **and 10 days to return any books you don't want to keep.**

There is no minimum number of books to buy,
and you may cancel membership at any time.
See back to sign up!

*Please include $2.00 for shipping and handling.

YES! ☐

Sign me up for the Leisure Western Book Club
and send my FOUR FREE BOOKS! If I choose to stay
in the club, I will pay only $14.00* each month,
a savings of $9.96!

NAME: _____

ADDRESS: _____

_____

TELEPHONE: _____

E-MAIL: _____

☐ **I WANT TO PAY BY CREDIT CARD.**

☐ VISA　　☐ MasterCard.　　☐ DISCOVER

ACCOUNT #: _____

EXPIRATION DATE: _____

SIGNATURE: _____

Send this card along with $2.00 shipping & handling to:

Leisure Western Book Club
20 Academy Street
Norwalk, CT 06850-4032

Or fax (must include credit card information!) to: 610.995.9274.
You can also sign up online at www.dorchesterpub.com.

*Plus $2.00 for shipping. Offer open to residents of the U.S. and Canada only.
Canadian residents please call 1.800.481.9191 for pricing information.
If under 18, a parent or guardian must sign. Terms, prices and conditions subject to change. Subscription subject
to acceptance. Dorchester Publishing reserves the right to reject any order or cancel any subscription.

JOIN NOW!

tight grasp on my reins, and mounted. The light was stronger and more direct, but the eastern horizon was a strange hue of crimson.

"Just might be rain comin'," Zeb observed.

"That'll slow us down, won't it?"

Stone glared at me as if I'd asked him if pigs could fly. "Rain would be the best thing that could happen," he said. "It wouldn't slow us down none to speak of, and it would cool out us an' our horses—an' it would wash away our tracks." He snorted in disgust. "Slow us down? Damn. For a schoolteacher, you sure ain't too bright, Pound."

"I never attended a class on how to elude a damned posse after murdering three people," I answered coldly.

Stone chuckled. "Don't go gettin' all feisty now," he said. "You need all your gumption for ridin'."

Stone spurred his horse into a jog, and I followed. It took an hour or so for my black to work the stiffness out of his muscles. Eventually, his gaits became less rigid and he covered ground calmly and evenly. We rode in the Indian fashion we'd used after the fiasco in Morgansville, although we shortened the gallop segment substantially. Two hours out, we came upon a scum-covered little water hole. The water was shallow, almost as warm as the air, and tasted brackish. Nevertheless, we filled our canteens, drank as much as we could hold, and let the horses suck as long as we dared. Stone had to literally haul his roan's head out of the water with his reins. He walked the horse ten yards or so and stood, staring east. The sky in that direction was a rolling, churning mass of dull-gray, ominous-looking clouds. Snake's tongues of lightning glinted, flickered for the briefest part of a second, and were gone. We felt rather than heard the deep grumble of thunder. I stopped my horse next to Zeb.

"Gonna be hell to pay when that hits," he said.

I decided I had to tell him. "Zeb—do you know what a phobia is?"

"Sure. Sick dog."

"No—that's hydrophobia. But a phobia—well, that's a fear, Zeb. A kind of fear that's bigger—worse—than a normal fear."

"Oh. So?"

"I have a phobia about storms, Zeb. I've had it for years, ever since I was a child. I thought I'd better let you know."

Zeb started his horse ahead. "That ain't so bad," he said. "Most folks is at lest a little bit scared of storms. I wouldn't worry about it, Pound."

I rode side by side with Zeb, checking the progress of the tempest in the sky behind us every few minutes.

It was beyond midday when we first noticed the drop in temperature of the gusty wind that had been at our backs most of the morning. The horses were nervous: The thunder was almost constant, and what earlier had been a low grumble became an insistent, evil growl that raised and dropped in pitch with each new burst from the sky. Lightning slashed through the charged air, its searing hiss audible over the thunder. I was shaking badly and my palms were dripping sweat. The horses, their fear more powerful than their fatigue, shook their heads wildly, attempting to get their bits in their teeth and run from the monster behind them. Stone sawed his reins, cursing, fighting his roan to a halt. He turned in his saddle to face the storm, his wild-eyed horse dancing and pawing the ground. I managed to grind my horse to a stop a few feet from Zeb, using the same, heavy-handed, sawing pressure on the reins. I was every bit as frightened as the horses. The fact that I knew the fear was irrational, bordering on the foolish, diminished it not at all. Moments passed, and stretched into minutes. I was just barely able to control my mount, and Stone was doing little better. He turned to me.

"Pound," he shouted over the wind, "see that black cloud—that one off to the left a bit, kinda by itself?"

My eyes followed Zeb's nod toward the storm. "I . . . I think I see the one you mean. Yes, I do. What about it?"

"Don't it look like a turtle what ain't got but three legs? See the head an' the shell? Damn, that's funny, ain't it?"

For the most fleeting speck of time, I considered killing him. Then I did the only thing I *could* do, the only thing that came to mind. I screamed as loud and as long as I was able, putting all my fear and anger and frustration into the shriek.

That did it for the horses. They reared in unison, got under their bits, and blasted away from the oncoming storm at a frenzied, maniacal gallop. Zeb was a stride ahead of me, and I saw him give his roan all the rein it wanted. I followed his lead and threw all my slack forward and let my horse do his damndest. We pounded across the scrub- and mesquite-covered ground like a pair of juggernauts from hell. We had no more control over our horses than we did over the tempest that was driving them. The wind slammed our backs with enough force to bend us far forward in our saddles, and the first drops of rain stung like pebbles fired from a slingshot. Then, suddenly, we were *in* the holocaust: It was on all sides—it was above and below us. The roar—the incredible, screaming din—deafened us. I closed my eyes and held on to my saddle horn with both hands. It was impossible to see anyway. The rain was a savage, living beast that buffeted and slammed us cruelly first in one direction, and then another, and then yet another.

Incredibly, the storm passed us as quickly as it had struck. Our horses slowed from their crazed gallop to a toe-dragging and exhausted walk in a matter of seconds, their sides heaving like enormous bellows. We watched, as soaking wet as if we'd gone swimming fully clothed, as the cataclysm hurtled away from us. The sun was aready warming us; directly above, the sky was blue.

Stone cleared his throat. "Uh . . . Pound?"

"What?" I answered from between teeth clenched so tightly my jaw hurt.

"Now, I don't mean nothin' by this. I'm just askin', you understand. So I'll know."

I couldn't take the spasms in my jaw any longer. I relaxed and took a deep breath. "What is it, Stone?" I asked wearily.

"You don't . . . uh . . . scream much like you just done, do you? I don't care—I just need to know. See, if you was to up an' scream like a old woman while we was takin' a bank or somethin', well, it could mess things up. See what I mean?"

"To the best of my knowledge," I said, trying to keep my voice level and controlled, "I've never screamed like that before. I doubt that I'll do it again. Satisfied?"

"Sure." Stone smiled at me. "You've got some strange ways about you, pard. You sure goosed the horses, though. I don't know when I've rode that fast before. Specially over ground like this—all poked through with prairie dog holes an' such."

"Do you have any idea why I screamed, Zeb?"

"Why? Hell no. Why did you?"

"Forget it," I said. "Forget it."

We rode at a walk for an hour. Once again, I had to admit that Zeb had a fine eye for horses. His roan and my black had been forced to work harder and longer than a man should demand of a horse, and they'd been panicked into a long and wild gallop that would most likely have dropped lesser animals. Yet, after a meandering walk that didn't strees them, both horses were ready to pick up the walk-lope-gallop pace again. We stopped whenever we struck what sorry water there was, although the storm had, if nothing else, sweetened the water to the degree that it was at least potable. We rested our horses periodically, and let them graze whenever we came across patches of buffalo grass. As dusk began to set in, Zeb cut the gallop from our rhythm of riding but didn't appear to be looking for a place to stop for the night. I asked him about this. We were riding at a walk, and he was rolling a cigarette.

"Here's how I see it," Zeb said. "We've been goin' real good. The storm washed out any tracks we was leavin'. 'Course, the lawman—if he's got more'n half a brain—must have knowed we was headed for Houston. But he can't be sure no more. He knows we can swing up to Dallas or Fort Worth or Wichita Falls now, without him knowin', 'cause he's lost our trail. He can send men out to see if they can cut our tracks, but he can't be sure about nothin' no more. The storm done us a big favor."

"*Did* us a favor, not done us a favor."

Zeb looked pained. "Dammit, Pound, are you gonna start that again?"

"Sorry," I admitted. "Maybe I spent too many years teaching and correcting the kind of grammatical foul-ups you tend to—"

"Anyways," Stone interrupted, as if I hadn't spoken, "it seems to me we should go right on to Houston an' do like we planned. There'll be close to a full moon tonight. I figure we ride right through the night an' then tomorrow, too. We should hit Houston tomorrow night."

I considered what Zeb had said. It made sense— good sense. "Fine with me. Can the horses take it?"

"Yeah. Leastwise, I think so. I hate to keep them movin', but we got no choice."

I learned that night and the next day how easy it is to sleep, or at least doze, in the saddle. Stone set the pace, and my horse followed his with little direction on my part. My chin would drop to my chest, my shoulders would hunch forward, and the gentle, rocking motion of my horse's stride would lull me into a light state of sleep. I suppose the principle— that of the rocking—is what puts an infant in a cradle to sleep. Zeb was able to get some rest also, but not nearly as much as I. He set the course and I—or my horse, to be more honest—followed. Zeb tried to point out the star he was using that night for a reference point. But, hard as I loooked, I couldn't distinguish the dot of light he was riding toward. All the stars looked pretty much the same to me. He gave up in disgust, mumbling and cursing about my lack of navigational skills.

I found myself jerking awake from vivid, sweaty dreams of the stagecoach the day before. In one such dream, both the woman and the boy pointed at me with outstretched hands. In another, the blood from the child's throat puddled and then pooled and then turned into an evil red wave that chased me just as the storm had earlier. The longer we rode, the farther apart such dreams occurred.

At daybreak, we gave the horses a couple of hours of rest. Their debilitation was obvious in the droop of their swollen eyelids and the lassitude of their movements. Zeb hobbled them and loosened but didn't remove the saddles. He went over each horse carefully, picking up each hoof and prying out pebbles that had become embedded in the horny tissue around the shoes with his pocketknife. Zeb spoke to the animals as if they were old friends who just happened to be horses. "Just a few more hours, boys," I heard him murmur. "A few more hours an' a few more miles an' you'll be chompin' prime oats an' chowin' down on hay so fresh an' sweet it ain't even dry yet. Damned if you won't, boys—you've earned that an' a whole lot more." His voice trailed off to a whisper so low I couldn't hear individual words. I stretched out on the still-cool and slightly dew-damp ground and fell asleep.

It seemed as if only minutes had passed when Zeb was nudging me awake. As I sat up, though, I saw the sun had done some climbing while I slept. Stone handed me four banded stacks of bills—two of twenties and two of fifties. I already put half the double eagles in your saddlebags," he said.

I was still groggy. "How much do we have?"

"Right about six thousand or so, close as I can figure. We've each got half, give or take a bit. Now look, Pound: Don't put your money in no hotel safe. Keep it somewhere you can get to it in a hurry, need be. Me, I'm keepin' mine in my room, under the mattress. Don't carry more'n a hundred or so with you. A man with too much money draws attention. I'll be stayin' at a place called the Carleton. You stay anywheres else. Let's plan on meetin' at O'Neill's two days after we get in. You get your new clothes an' haircut soon's you can. Keep outta the booze. An' don't . . ."

I cut him off. "Don't worry about me, Zeb, and don't be so damned condescending. I'll take care of myself. I suggest that you stay away from the poker tables, and that you keep the barrel of your pistol out of other people's noses, as well as—"

"What's that mean?" Stone interrupted.

"What does what mean?"

"Conversending. You just said it: conversending."

"That's con*de*scending. It means—well, talking down to a person. Treating an adult as a child, just as you were doing a few moments ago."

"Oh," Stone said. "Damn. I didn't mean nothin' by it. I was only tryin' to help you out, is all. Well. We'd best tighten our cinches an' ride." Zeb began removing the hobbles from the horses' forelegs.

"Pound," he said, his back to me.

"Yes?"

"I . . ."

I was anxious to get moving, but Stone had not yet mounted. "Come on, Zeb. What's the problem?"

"You've been in lots of schools, right? Colleges an' such?"

I sighed. "Yes. A few."

Zeb kept his back to me, even though the hobbles were off the horses and he'd set his cinch. "Maybe you can answer me a question." He spoke slowly, picking his words carefully. "How bad," he asked, "is a man supposed to feel after he's gunned down a man or two or even . . ." The word "even" hung in the air. The face of the child I'd killed flashed in my mind. I pulled my cinch tight and put the money in my saddlebags.

"I think," I said, "a person is supposed to feel a great deal worse than we do, Zeb. A great deal worse."

"Yeah," Stone said. "I kinda thought so."

We had lived on beef jerky, bad water, and moldy

crackers for the past four days. Now, on the last stretch to Houston, I began to fantasize about a very thick, blood-rare steak, of such proportions that it hung off a large plate all the way around. Next to the steak I saw a schooner of beer with a creamy-white head, so cold that drops of condensation ran down the sides of the mug. I tried to erase the image of the beer from my mind but didn't have much success. I smiled to myself, rather mournfully. The steak I'd have—but the thought of beer was as close as I intended to get to it. That decision, however, didn't make the schooner in my mind any less attractive.

The sun climbed higher and gathered strength, beating down upon us with its heavy, oppressive, energy-killing fervor. Zeb once again dropped the gallop from our sequence. We rode on, mile after mile, alternating between a fast walk and a slow lope. It seemed to me that I'd never been anywhere but on the back of a black horse, riding across a prairie that had no end, toward a place that couldn't be reached. I wondered if Zeb and I were in hell, and if the journey would carry on forever, punishing us for all eternity.

Miraculously, unbelievably, the sun reached and passed its zenith and its power began to diminish. Zeb kept the horses at a walk. I dozed, the vision of the steak and beer taunting me.

"Pound."

My chin snapped up from my chest. It was dusk. "What?"

"You ride on in," Zeb said. "The town's maybe six or eight miles straight ahead. You can't miss it—

you'll be ridin' in right on Main Street. We're gettin' too close to be together. I'm gonna swing out an' around an' come in the opposite end. I'll see you in two days in O'Neill's. You remember all you got to do? I ain't raggin' on you. I just need to make sure."

"I know you're not. I remember it all. I'll see you in a couple of days in O'Neill's."

"Good luck."

"Yeah," I said. "Good luck to you, too."

Chapter Seven

I rode on alone, following a rutted path that could be called a road only because it was ten or twelve feet wide and seemed to lead somewhere. It was strange riding without Zeb. As I drew closer to Houston, I unbuckled my gunbelt and holster and placed them in my right saddlebag. Although I'd carried the side arm only a short period of time, I missed the weight of the weapon, the physical sensation of having it at my side. I felt oddly weak and vulnerable without my Smith & Wesson at hand, as if I needed it to prove my potency, my worth. The idea of forming a judgment of a man predicated upon his ability to draw quickly and to hit what (or whom) he was firing at, was, at one time, abhorrent to me. Now I wasn't so sure. In a sense, I'd become a different man since I'd begun carrying the pistol. Without it, I'd been the town drunk, a contemptible figure, a man who could do nothing and was nothing. Armed, I was Zeb Stone's partner. I'd become instantaneously wealthy, making far more in the few minutes it took to rob a bank than I'd make in five or even ten years of teaching.

Further, I'd become sober since I'd begun carrying a weapon, and I was proud of what I'd accomplished in terms of my addiction to alcohol. As I thought about it, it seemed to me that my personality—the things that made me who I am—were at the crux of my need for alcohol. I found it interesting how I'd traded booze for Dr. Oliver's swill in such a rapid and facile manner. I decided I'd have to watch my handling of *anything* that made me feel good, from whiskey to medicine to even food and sex.

Porter Stillman, a clerk in Burnt Rock, was hugely fat, and yet he was almost constantly eating. I guessed that my alcohol intake wasn't much different from Porter's need to stuff himself with food long after any real appetite must have been extinguished. My prior misuse of booze had many parallels with Stillman's food intake. But—and this was a very big but—I was no longer drinking.

My thoughts flashed from that last one to the fact that I'd become something else since I became Zeb's partner: I'd become a killer—and worse even than that, the killer of a child. I realized that I'd never, for the rest of my life, forget what I'd done.

The first structure at the north end of Houston's Main Street was a livery stable. I reined in, dismounted, and led my black into the lantern-lighted alley between the long rows of stalls. A young man—perhaps seventeen or so—stepped out of the small office. He wore his sandy-blond hair shoulder length, and he was dressed in a buckskin jacket with foolishly long fringe and a pair of gray pin-striped trousers tucked into the tops of gleamingly polished black boots. He also wore a pair of Colts with bone grips, turned butt-forward in his holsters. His resemblance to Buffalo Bill Cody was astounding, and the boy obviously played upon that likeness. There was a Ned Buntline novel—*Buffalo Bill at Bloody Arrow Pass*—opened covers-up on the top of the small desk behind which the youth had been sitting. He looked me over with irritating, heavy-lidded insolence.

"Yeah?" he asked.

"I want this horse rubbed down—tonight. Now. Give him a double ration of oats and a half-bale of your best hay each day. Start his grain tonight, but don't feed it all at once. Get a blacksmith in here tomorrow to trim his hooves and shoe him all the way around. Make sure the smith doesn't reset the old shoes. I want four new ones, with a caulk at each toe. Understood?"

"Well," the boy drawled, "that's one mighty big order, pardner. I reckon I can handle everything but the rub. The kid who cleans the stalls and exercises and rubs down the horses won't be here until morning."

Both the drawl and the speech were directly from the pen of Ned Buntline.

"You do it." I began removing my saddlebags from behind my cantle.

"Me?" The boy smirked, shifting the long blade of hay upon which he was nibbling from one side of his mouth to the other.

"I don't reckon you're reading my smoke signals, pardner. I don't rub no horses. My pa owns this place." He rested the palms of his hands on the bone grips of his weapons. His stance, his arrogance, his mindless defiance, reminded me very acutely of students of mine who had backed me down and then laughed in my face about it.

I took a twenty-dollar bill from my pocket and handed it to the boy. At the same time, I pulled the piece of hay from his mouth and dropped it to the dirt floor. His eyes widened and then hardened, narrowing to angry slits. He began to say something. I grabbed his nose between my thumb and forefinger and pulled his face within a pair of inches of mine.

"You rub this horse down tonight, Buffalo Bill," I said, "because if I stop back here and he hasn't been cared for, I'll cut your pretty hair to your scalp and then make you eat it—and I'll jam those two pistols right where they belong—sideways. Is that quite clear?"

"Yeah."

I twisted his nose. Tears of pain made his eyes blurry and indistinct. "Yes—yessir," he said in a heavily nasal tone of voice. I pushed the boy backward with enough force so that he stumbled and banged into a closed stall door, shoulder first.

"My name is Wordsworth," I said, "Bill Wordsworth. You'll be taking care of my horse for two—maybe three weeks. I'll be checking on you. I don't want a stable hand or your father to work with my horse. I want you to do it—then I'll know where to come if I have any complaints." The boy wouldn't meet my eyes, but he nodded his head and mumbled, "Yessir . . ." I walked out of the stable with my saddlebags over my shoulder.

Damn, I thought, that felt good. *Very* good.

I walked half a block and hustled into the first restaurant I came upon. It's been said that the pleasure of anticipation often far exceeds the actuality, the consummation of the fantasy. My meal contradicted that little piece of philosophy. The steak was every bit as delicious as I'd dreamed it would be. I drank several tall glasses of ice-cold buttermilk with the steak and potatoes, and a pot of coffee afterward. The restaurant had a bar. I avoided looking at the bottles and the men who were drinking there. I couldn't, however, avoid hearing the drunken, imbecilic conversations and the braying laughter.

I almost had convinced myself that beer was a separate and distinct matter, and that whiskey was my problem, not beer. *Almost*—but not quite. I was kidding myself, and I knew it. I'd gotten stumbling, vomiting drunk many times on beer. It wasn't the specific beverages I needed to avoid, it was alcohol.

As I sipped at my final cup of steaming-hot coffee, I planned on how to best carry out my charade. I already had a name—Bill Wordsworth. I needed an occupation. After some deliberation, I decided to become a land speculator. I leaned back in my chair, sated and at peace. All I required were clothes, a haircut, and a hotel room, and my transformation would be complete.

I found the difference between Houston and San

Antonio to be a matter of degree. Houston was larger, brighter, and more noisy, but the stores, restaurants, and saloons seemed interchangeable. The wooden plank sidewalks were crowded with pedestrian traffic, and men on horseback threaded their ways through groups of people on the street. The occasional fluent and highly imaginative cursing of a drover hauling a load of various goods—bricks, lumber, barrels of beer, crates of hardware—had no noticeable effect on those being denounced for blocking the street with their phaetons, buggies, and farm wagons.

The main window of Dalton's General Store featured what appeared to be a good selection of men's suits. My glance settled upon a Clay Worsted with a matching vest. I'd worn Clay suits before exchanging teaching for boozing, and I'd found them to be of excellent quality.

The first sound I heard as I stepped into Dalton's was the unmelodious clank of a cheap bell, activated by my opening of the door. The second sound, a very familiar voice, came from the rear of the store.

"Don't condersend me, you puny little maggot!" Stone bellowed. "I just might *like* my drawers a little short!"

I hurried down the aisle. Stone stood, red-faced, in a suit coat that could easily have accommodated him and another person his size, and a pair of matching trousers that left a two-inch band of milky-white skin between the tops of his boots and the cuffs of the pants. An elderly, frightened clerk whose bald head glistened with perspiration was edging away from my partner. I glared at Stone. As he caught my eyes, he became suddenly sheepish.

"Look," he said to the clerk, "you pick out the damned suit an' the size—I ain't got the time to mess around here no longer."

The clerk, very obviously relieved, lost some of his fear-induced pallor. I spun on my heel and left Dalton's. Damn it, I thought, there must have been fifteen stores in Houston that carry men's clothing, and I had to pick the same one my boneheaded partner chose. Stone's shooting off his mouth bothered me. Someone as belligerent as he was would attract attention. Zeb was about as civilized as a hawk. I decided to tear into him when we met at O'Neill's, if he lasted for two days without being jailed or gunned down.

I chose a suit from a rack at the next mercantile down the block. The fit was good. I bought the suit, a vest, seven Forbes white shirts, a silver pocket watch and chain, several sets of city-type undergarments, and a Remington double derringer .41 with a three-inch barrel. The two-shot pistol fit neatly in the right pocket of my suit coat. I selected a pair of black Congress Brand shoes and had the clerk wrap my purchases in a single bundle in brown paper. There was a barbershop three doors beyond the store. As I waited my turn for a bath, I paged through the ragged pile of newspapers provided by the barber for his customers. The headline of a four-day-old *San Antonio Clarion* struck me an unexpected blow in the stomach. My hands trembled as I read the story.

CHILD, DRIVER, GUARD SLAIN
DURING STAGE ROBBERY ATTEMPT

Two desperadoes attacked and killed the driver and guard of a Moore Coach Line vehicle en route to San Antonio yesterday. The gunsels coldheartedly fired several shots into the small body of James Turnwell, Jr., age five. Mrs. Isiah Turnwell, the mother of the slain infant, was not injured.

Both the driver, Harlan Lester, age 41, of San Antonio, and Sam Starling, age about 45, permanent address unknown, were killed by gunshot wounds sustained while they were valiantly trying to defend their passengers.

Payson Moore, president of Moore Coach Lines, made the following statement: "The perpetrators of this vicious and heinous act must be apprehended and punished. To this end, I am posting a one-thousand-dollar reward for the capture or death of either of the two malfeasors involved."

The San Antonio Clarion applauds Mr. Moore. Mrs. Turnwell, understandably overwrought after her ordeal, was unable to give comprehensive descriptions of the killers. She told San Antonio sheriff Raymond Myers that she heard the name "Pound" mentioned by one of the thugs in addressing the other. Sheriff Myers told *The Clarion* that he and his posse lost the trail of the robbers due to an unexpected rainstorm which washed away the tracks Myers and his men were following. The Sheriff believes the cowardly pair may have been heading toward Houston.

Law officials believe that the two . . .

"Sir? Sir?"

I lowered the paper. The barber was standing in front of me. "Your bath is poured and . . . Sir? Are you sick or something?"

I folded the newspaper first page inward and tossed it on the table. "Nothing serious," I said. "It's my heart. Every so often, it skips a beat and I lose my color for a minute—that's all." I did my best to smile. "It's a damned inconvenience."

I followed the barber into the back room and set my package and my saddlebags on the floor next to the tub. I soaked and scrubbed for half an hour and then toweled dry and dressed in my new clothing and shoes. I had the barber cut my hair quite short. He was a talkative, gossipy type of man.

"Hell of a thing over there near San Antone, wasn't it?" he said, his scissors poised in his hand. "How do you want it cut? You don't have much length now. Looks look you got a haircut not too long ago."

"I did. I've decided I want to wear it a bit shorter all the way around. And I'd like to see if you can put some shape to my beard. I've only gone a few days without shaving, but I thought I'd try a Vandyke, just to see how it looks."

The barber went to work. "Like I said, that was a hell of a thing over by San Antonio, wasn't it."

"What's that?" I asked. "I'm not sure I know what you're talking about."

"I thought you was reading the story in the *Clarion*. Couple of men shot hell out of a stagecoach and killed the driver and shotgunner and a little boy."

"Oh," I said. "Yes. A terrible thing."

"A rope is too good for them two robbers. The stage company has a thousand dollars on each of them. Seems to me, that ain't enough. The whole thing makes me wonder what this country's coming to."

I grunted, indicating agreement, hoping the barber would shut the hell up and do his job.

"Now," he went on, "I figure it like this. Right after the Great War, we had them Quantrell's Raiders riding and raising hell and killing every innocent person they come across. See, I heard most of them men saw heavy fighting during the war and all that fighting just plain made them crazy, and they couldn't stop after Appomatox. I figure the two who gunned the baby are the same. But that don't give them a reason to do what they done, that's for sure. Yep, they're crazy, Okay. Best thing for them is a bullet—and they'll get that, just as sure as you're born. Two thousand dollars is a lot of money. The bounty hunters ain't going to let that go by. Not by a long shot. You mark my words, friend: Those two gunsels ain't got a full month to live. You watch and see if I ain't right." He paused, waiting for a response from me.

"You're probably right," I said, doing my best to sound casual and only vaguely interested.

" 'Course I am. Scum like them ain't fit to live. Oops! Sorry—did I nick you?"

I'd flinched involuntarily when the barber stated so flatly that Zeb and I weren't fit to draw breath. "No," I said. "Just a little twinge, is all. Say—can you speed it up a bit? I'd appreciate it. I have lots of business to conduct, and I'd like to get to it."

"Sure," the barber said without taking any offense. "I get to running my mouth at times. See, I like people and I like to talk, so barbering is a ideal job for me."

I grunted again, without speaking. He finished me up without another word.

Afterword, I inspected myself in a large handheld mirror. My new suit and vest, stiff white shirt, gleaming black shoes, shorn hair, and well-started Vandyke beard combined to make me look like a new man. I smiled into the mirror. It was exactly the effect I wanted. I paid the barber, tipped him moderately, and left, my entire old outfit—Stetson included—wrapped in brown paper. I dropped the package into a trash barrel in an alley between a dress shop and a restaurant. The thought struck me that I'd thrown away more clothes in the past couple of weeks than I'd owned for the last two years.

Pound was no more. From his ashes had risen Bill Wordsworth, land speculator.

I took a room at the Houston Hotel and paid for two weeks in advance. The clerk who signed me in and gave me my receipt barely looked at me. The room was comfortable, although somewhat spartan. I had a decent-sized bed, a three-drawer dresser, a straight-backed chair, and a washstand. There was a porcelain slop bucket on the floor under my window. I'd specified first-floor accommodations. It's substantially less difficult to exit in a hurry from a first-floor room than it is to jump from the second or third floor.

Although I was tired—bone-weary, in fact—the noise and the action in the street was contagious. I knew I'd be unable to sleep, so I decided to treat myself to a walking tour of the grand city of Houston, Texas. I stopped in front of the first saloon I came to and on impulse decided to go in.

The polished mahogany bar in Zimmerman's Retreat for Gentlemen was quite long—probably forty feet or so—and was being tended by three men dressed identically in Prince Albert suits. The lighting was excellent, and the large lanterns were hung well up on the walls and ceiling beams, cutting the glare that was so evident in most saloons. Shiny brass spittoons were placed every five feet along the length of the bar. There were eight or ten poker tables, but no roulette wheel. The place was, without a doubt, the finest drinking hall I'd ever visited.

The dimensions of both the painting and the nude herself in the composition hung above the neat line of bottles behind the bar were staggering. I felt a vague but pleasant stirring below my belt. It had been a long, long time. I decided it wasn't going to be too much longer.

The men in the bar were dressed much as I was. There were no grimy ranch hands stinking of cattle manure and long-unwashed clothing. Although the place was crowded, the noise level was relatively low. A young Negro dressed in an elegant black tuxedo and a brilliant red cummerbund played sudued, restrained little pieces on a grand piano. I noticed that there was an elevated area—a stage—a few feet behind the pianist. In the center of the stage was a nicely lettered sign resting on what appeared to be an artist's easel. The sign proclaimed:

ZIMMERMAN'S RETREAT
FOR GENTLEMEN
presents
MISS SALLY LOVE
internationally renowned
singer, dancer, and entertainer
two performances nightly

When I turned from reading the sign, I found a bartender directly across from me.

"Your pleasure, sir?" he asked. The bottles on the shelf directly under the nude were calling to me. The various shades of amber and mahogany of the whiskeys, bourbons, and ryes caught my eyes and refused to let me look away. My throat performed swallowing motions, although my mouth was dry. There was a tall schooner of beer on the bar between me and the bartender. I could actually smell the tangy scent of the beer and imagined how it would feel going down my throat and spreading its familiar warmth through my system. Saying "Nothing just now" was one of the most difficult things I've ever done, but that's exactly what I did.

It was abundantly clear that I shouldn't have come into the saloon in the first place. I stood quite still attempting to gather my wits enough to walk out and continue my tour of Houston.

The two gentlemen next to me were discussing—not arguing—the merits of the Thoroughbred horse as contrasted to the celebrated abilities of the Texas Short Horse. I'd been with Zeb Stone long enough so that any logical, civilized conversation was as sweet as white sugar to me. In motioning for another drink, the fellow next to me inadvertently jostled my shoulder.

"Pardon me, friend," he said.

"Pardon me" in a saloon? I *liked* that place.

"I couldn't help overhearing parts of your conversation," I said. "I wonder if I may offer a viewpoint?"

"Certainly," the second man answered, "but only with the stipulation that you join us in a taste of the fine Kentucky bourbon Mr. Zimmerman serves."

My thoughts suddenly accelerated like a runaway locomotive. One drink, I thought. One damned drink can't do me any harm. I *won't* get drunk. At the same time, a clamoring voice in my head was telling me over and over, "There's no such thing as one drink for you—you *will* get drunk. You'll destroy what you've gained."

The gentleman at my side looked at me inquisitively, obviously wondering why I hadn't responded to his offer. My palms were suddenly dripping wet. These men, this place, the conversation, and the bottles and the beer—I wanted to run, flee the place, be physically away. What I'd told Zeb and what I'd told myself rang in my ears.

Just one, I promised myself. *Just one.*

I nodded affirmatively. "I've always had a warm spot in my heart for good bourbon," I said. My voice sounded hollow and sad, even to me. I swallowed hard and dredged up a comment Zeb had made from my memory and translated it into the English language. "Now, as to horses," I said, my voice already stronger and more confident, "it's been my experience that the cross of Thoroughbred and Short Horse blood almost invariably produces an animal superior to both its sire and its dam. Although I rarely ride horseback for extended periods of time, men in my employ swear by the cross I've just mentioned for speed, endurance, and temperament."

I tilted my head and knocked back the generous shot of bourbon. It went down as easily as cool, fresh cream and began to work its magic even before I lowered the glass. I motioned to the bartender. I thoroughly enjoyed my conversation with my two aquaintances, both of whom were traveling hardware salesmen. We discovered that we had much in common to discuss and many similar interests.

When I awakened the following morning, I was completely nude except for my left shoe, flat on my back in my bed at the Houston Hotel. My mouth tasted as if I'd eaten a long-dead prairie dog. My head thudded, crashed, with each beat of my pulse. Automatically, I reached under my pillow. There was no bottle.

"Damn you," I croaked out loud. "Damn you, Pound."

Bits and fragments of the night before began to sift

their way through the lancing, searing pain in my head. A face flashed in my mind but receded too quickly for me to recognize the features. It flashed again. Sally Love. The face was that of Sally Love: pudgy, eyes set too closely together, teeth like those of a bull buffalo. I could see the woman clearly. She had a great deal of hair in her nose. Her stage makeup appeared to have been applied by a barn painter. Her hair smelled like bacon gone bad, and was plastered into a bun-type affair with what felt like axle lubricant. I'd given her money—two tens or two twenties, I couldn't recall which.

I brought my hand to my face. It trembled as if I'd never stopped drinking, as if I'd been drunk instead of sober every day since I'd stopped. My stomach churned and acidic bile rose its burning way from my gut up into my throat.

I'd let Zeb down. I'd let our partnership down. I'd let myself down. I closed my eyes, but sleep wouldn't come.

Never again, I promised myself. *Never again.* I'd done well. I could do it again. I *knew* I could. Even my short period of sobriety had changed my life. I had been physically in better shape than I'd been in years. I was sure I could do it again. I decided that Zeb didn't need to know of my relapse. As far as I could recall, I'd gotten into no trouble, and I was sure I hadn't spoken with anyone other than the two gentlemen in Zimmerman's and Sally Love.

Perhaps, I thought, getting drunk this time had been necessary to prove to myself that I couldn't drink like other people. I realized that, and I believed it as much as I'd ever believed anything. There was absolutely no doubt in my mind that my addiction could never be extinguished. The best I could do was to hold it at bay, to refuse to give in to it. Maybe by going backward I had, in a paradoxical sense, actually moved ahead to a full realization that I would never be able to drink again with any degree of safety.

At least, I thought, my extended period of celibacy was over. I'd been able to function as a man. I felt good about that. I closed my eyes again, trying to recapture the blessed peace of sleep.

It was then that the itching—the fiery and incredibly intense and demanding itching—began.

Chapter Eight

Zeb and I stood side by side at the bar in O'Neill's. I'd spent the previous day and night scratching and groaning.

Stone made a fair appearance in a dark suit and matching vest. He'd decided upon a full-face beard, and it was growing in nicely. His hair was as short as mine but was parted in a meandering line down the center of his scalp. In several places shocks of hair stood erect, like miniature sheaves of wheat. He had a supercilious, smug little grin on his face.

"Gotta be crotch crickets," he said. "Ain't you somethin'? Damn."

"Look," I snarled, "if you're going to make light of me or ride me the way you've been doing, I'll go elsewhere for help. I don't find a bit of humor in this situation. My privates are literally bleeding from me digging at them with my fingernails, and yet you . . ."

Stone put his hand on my shoulder. "Sorry, pard. Anybody can get the little fellers. But you got nothin' to worry about. I'll tell you just exactly how to get rid of them. Now—listen up real close, so you don't miss nothin'. First, you buy yourself a big bottle of laudanum. Next, get one of them big, two-gallon pails—the kind with the handle. Then you buy a hefty book. It don't matter who wrote it, as long as it's big an' heavy. You with me so far?"

I looked around the saloon and scratched surreptitiously. "Go on," I said, "I'm with you: a bottle of laudanum, a two-gallon bucket with a handle, and a heavy book. What next?"

"Then," Zeb snickered, "you drop your drawers, drink the bottle of laudanum, an' beat hell out of the crabs with the pail. The book is for in case you get bored." Zeb broke into whinnying, horselike laughter. I walked out of O'Neill's without speaking another word to him, and didn't see him again for a week. It took me that long to cool down.

Early that afternoon a young, myopic physician examined me and sold me a bottle of milky-white liquid with which to drench the infected areas until the itching was gone. He charged me four dollars for the liquid and the exam. I'd have gladly paid a thousand.

"Perhaps," the doctor said, "rather than pursue the dubious carnal pleasures that can lead only to the fires of hell, your time would be better spent in more worthwhile pursuits."

"Perhaps," I said, not totally in disagreement with him. "I'll give it some thought."

I spent the rest of that day and all of the night pouring the liquid on myself every hour on the hour. I had no difficulty staying awake: I was alternating between periods of acute, unrelenting itching and the fiery anguish that accompanied each dose of the medication. It worked, though. Afterward, I slept a full thirty hours.

I came across Sally Love in a restaurant about a week after I'd gotten over my infestation. She was alone at a table. I sat down across from her.

"Well," she beamed through what looked like a few pounds of makeup, "if it ain't the ol' stud horse. I was thinkin' you up an' forgot me."

"You gave me bugs," I growled. "They nearly drove me insane."

Sally met my eyes and smiled demurely—or as close to being demure as a lice-ridden heifer such as she could become. "No extra charge, ol' horse," she said. "The pets are free to my favorite customers. Wanna give another herd a home?"

I'm rarely at a loss for words. Just then, I was. I sputtered a bit and stomped away from her table, red-faced with both anger and embarrassment. Just before I slammed the door behind me, I heard her laughter. I stood outside on the sidewalk for a long moment. Then I couldn't help it. I broke into laughter myself.

The days in Houston passed in an uneventful but nevertheless pleasant monotony that demanded nothing of me. I slept as long as I cared to in the morning and took my breakfast at one of several restaurants I found that served good food in man-sized portions. Often I walked to the stable to make sure the young fellow with the Buffalo Bill fixation was taking proper care of my horse. Afternoons I'd sit in front of my hotel in the wooden chairs provided for guests and/or loafers, smoke a cigar, and read newspapers. If the sun was strong and I was feeling languorous, I'd go to my room for a nap. I met Zeb at O'Neill's frequently in the evening. I drank nothing alcoholic and felt good about that. The barkeep at O'Neill's had even stopped asking what I wanted and, instead, would nod to me and take Zeb's order. I was generally in bed before eleven. I'd hardly dented my cache of money, yet I was living higher than I ever had before.

Thoughts of the boy outside of San Antonio still plagued me, but not with the terrible immediacy they had shortly after the incident. I'd analyzed every second of the attempted robbery, and I'd come to the conclusion that I'd simply acted in an effort to save my partner's life. That the outcome of my act was terribly, flagrantly wrong, there could be no doubt. And the death of the youngster was a tragedy that would be with me forever. But I would have done the same thing again, given the same circumstances. I had no way of knowing the rifle was a toy. I was guilty of murder—but it was a murder that arose from a horrible mistake, not from anger or malice on my part.

All that, I knew, didn't make the boy any less dead, nor did it mitigate his mother's anguish and pain.

Zeb and I sat at a table in O'Neill's, discussing our plans. He was pouring shots from a bottle and drinking them more rapidly than was usual for him. He seemed down, sullen, listless. He drank mechanically, averting his eyes from mine by staring either at his bottle or at the wall above and behind me.

"What's wrong, Zeb?" I asked.

"Me?" He tried to look surprised. "What makes you think there's somethin' wrong?"

"Several things: The way you're drinking. The way you won't look me in the eye."

Zeb sighed deeply. "Well," he said. "Damn. Here's the thing, Pound: I ain't got but four dollars left. My money run out on me. I can't even get my horse outta the stable 'cause I ain't paid his care."

I had to digest that for a good long time. It seemed impossible to me that Zeb could be out of funds. "You spent three *thousand* dollars in three weeks? On what, Zeb? What did you buy?"

"I . . . uhh . . . pkr," Stone mumbled.

"What? Speak up, dammit!"

"Poker, Pound. Poker! I didn't have nothin' else to do, so I sat in on a few games. It ain't like we can't get more money. The damn state is full of banks. Damn, Pound, how you do pick at a man!"

A fellow at the bar glanced our way as soon as Zeb said "Pound."

"Zeb," I said, "you're going to hang us. Don't call me by name. Think before you speak." The gent at the bar turned back to his drink. "Let me ask you something, Zeb. How in the name of all that's good and holy were you able to support yourself playing cards if you dropped three thousand in three weeks here in Houston?"

"Well, I did an awful lot of cheating. But the gamblers here are too sharp for me. The whole damn bunch of them are as crooked as a hound's back leg. I'm right sick of Houston, is what I am. I want to hit the trail an' pick up twenty-five thousand dollars an' go to Mexico, just like we talked about. I ain't a man to set still, doin' nothin'. I'm ready to ride. It's a wonder them fancy gamblin' men didn't condersend me outta my horse an' boots, too. Damn bloodsuckers."

"You've got the meaning of . . . nuts. Forget it."

Zeb looked confused. "Huh?"

"Nothing," I said. "Nothing. Where do we go from here?"

"North an' west," Stone answered, leaning over the table toward me, his voice low. "Two cowtowns, Silver Ridge an' Paris, are maybe a day—"

"Paris?" I asked.

"Paris, Texas, not Paris, England. Damn, Pound, for a schoolteacher you—"

"Go on," I interrupted. "Tell me the plan and keep the other comments to yourself."

"Anyways," Zeb continued, "Silver Ridge is maybe two days' ride, but we can make Paris from here in five, six hours. We can knock over two banks in one day, an' then pull for Waco an' rest up a bit before goin' on. Hell, there ain't nothin' but rattlers an' buffalo grass an' the Colorado River between Paris an' Waco. I seen it on a map. We'll run onto a few pissant towns, but nothin' that's too likely to have a bank. If we come across a place that does have a bank, we'll go ahead an' rob it. But I know Silver Ridge an' Paris have 'em. Okay?"

"When?" I asked.

Zeb leaned back in his chair. "Well," he said, "settin' here ain't puttin' nothin' in our pokes. I don't see no sense in wastin' more time. How's tomorrow, early mornin'? We can meet at the south end of Main Street, where I come into Houston. I'll tell you what, pard: It'll feel just fine to get outta this here suit an' into some trail clothes with my Colt by my side, where it belongs. I feel like a edgy ol' woman carryin' this toy I got in my pocket."

"I know what you mean," I agreed. "Mine feels—"

"*You* got a hideout too?" Stone interrupted.

I nodded. "Sure. I bought it the first night in town. It's a little two-shot derringer .41."

"Damn," Zeb said incredulously, "you sure do take to this outlawin' stuff."

I checked the room to make sure no one was paying any attention to us and then handed Zeb several fifty-dollar bills. "This should take care of everything," I said.

Stone nodded his thanks, pushed back his chair, and left O'Neill's. I lit a cigar.

Zeb had been right, I decided. It was time to ride. The stage incident was almost a month behind us. Our beards had changed our faces, and we'd both put on weight. We were different men. I'd checked the papers daily but failed to find a follow-up story to the piece I'd read in the barbershop. I thought it quite possible that Zeb's fear had caused him to overstate the danger we faced. And, quite frankly, I was as bored as Zeb with Houston. I missed the action of the trail. A thought struck me and I smirked. Perhaps bank robbery was addicting—most of the other things I liked were.

I sauntered down the walk to Dalton's, puffing on my cigar. I'd grown quite fond of Key West Cubans and planned to carry a box of fifty in my saddlebags.

The bell over the door at Dalton's clunked as I walked in. Business was slow. A clerk—not the same one with whom Zeb had the altercation—was leaning against the counter, talking with a square-shouldered gent whose back was to me. The clerk looked my way. I waved my hand, indicating that I was in no hurry. He nodded and returned to his conversation. As I picked up a pair of denim pants, a thick, grating voice sawed through the dusty silence of the store.

"I doubt they was together," the voice rasped, "but I'm damned near sure they're in Houston. They'd have come in three weeks or a few days more ago, and they'd probably be buying clothes to change their looks. I'm gonna be checkin' every store in Houston. Somebody *had* to see them."

"Sorry, Sheriff," the clerk said. "But I don't recall seeing nobody like you described. That don't mean they ain't been in here, though. I see a lots of faces every day, and it's hard to remember anything special about any of them. And another thing: I don't work at night. You might want to talk to the ol' coot who clerks nights."

"What's his name?"

"Dalton—same as mine." The clerk chuckled.

142

"He's my pa. He's sleeping just now—he does every afternoon, and then works until closing."

"I'll be back," the sheriff said. "If you see him before I do, tell him I want to talk to him." The sheriff paused. "And I'll tell you this, boy—any son of mine ever called me an old coot, I'd boot him from here to next Wednesday."

The clerk lost his smile. "Yessir. Mr. Dalton'll be glad to help you out if he can. A rope is too good for them kid-killers, Sheriff."

"I never said nothin' about a rope, now, did I?" the hoarse voice responded. "Them two are *mine*." Heavy boots thudded to the door. I heard the clank of the bell. I stood stock-still, breathing deeply until my heart stopped pounding so wildly. I grabbed pants, a shirt, a pair of boots, and a hat. When I was sure my hands and voice were under control, I walked over to the clerk.

"Howdy," he smiled.

I nodded. "Afternoon. I guess this will do it for today," I said, placing the goods on the counter.

"That fella there, with the big scar on his neck," the clerk volunteered, "is hunting them outlaws who shot up the stage and killed the little boy outside San Antone."

"Oh?"

"Yeah. Scary son of a gun. I wouldn't want him doggin' me, I'll tell you that for true."

"No," I agreed. "Neither would I."

I went directly to my hotel, paid my bill, fetched my saddlebags from under the bed, and stuffed my

143

new trail clothes into them. I tried to keep the hurry out of my stride as I walked to the stable.

Young Buffalo Bill was sitting on a bench in front, half asleep in the bright sun.

"Figure my bill and saddle my horse," I said.

The youth got up reluctantly and began to shuffle into the barn. I booted him in the rear. "Move," I said. He hustled down the row of stalls and returned leading my horse. The black's coat gleamed from daily brushing, and his muscles were tight and well-defined. The boy had worked him hard enough each day to raise a sweat—on both himself and my horse.

"You're owin' thirteen dollars, Mr. Wordsworth," the boy said.

I handed him a fifty-dollar bill. He gaped at it. "I can't change—"

I cut him off. "I didn't ask for change. Keep it. You did a good job." The boy pulled the cinch and bitted my horse as I laced my saddlebags behind the cantle. I made sure we were alone in the stable.

"Boy," I asked, "has anyone been snooping around here, asking questions?"

He looked bewildered. "Questions? Nossir. I ain't seen nobody askin' questions."

"Fine. Someone may come to see you. If you give him any information—any at all—I'll hear about it, and I'll come back. Is that clear?"

"Yeah . . . yessir. It's clear."

"Repeat it."

The young man's Adam's apple bobbed up and down like a yo-yo on a short string. His voice was shaky. "If . . . I answer any questions or say anything about you, you'll come back after me."

I mounted. "Okay. Make sure you stick to that. And I'll tell you something you might want to keep in mind: Being dead lasts an awful long time."

"Ye . . . yessir."

I rode to the Carleton and tied my horse to the hitching rail in front. Zeb was in room 107. I charged down the hallway and was about to rap on the door when I heard a feminine voice and then Zeb's raucous laughter from within the room.

Damn, I thought. Why is Stone's timing *always* so poor?

I knocked sharply. There was a silence in the room for a few moments, and then Zeb's voice boomed out, "Whoever it is, go away."

I knocked again. Bedsprings creaked. "Dammit," Stone shouted, "get the hell away from my door!"

"It's me—Mr. Wordsworth," I said. "I have to discuss the business deal we agreed upon earlier in the day. There've been some important changes." There were some mumbled curses I couldn't quite hear. Then Stone threw the door open. I stepped inside and closed it. Zeb stood there nude, a lopsided grin on his face. A red-haired lady in the bed pulled the sheet up to her chin, covering herself.

"Get rid of her," I said. "We have to talk." Zeb's eyes met mine and held. He wasn't too drunk to see that there was trouble. I gave him a twenty-dollar bill. He padded over to the bed and handed the money to the woman.

"Time for you to go," he said.

The woman pouted. "You said we'd—"

"Out. Now. Party's over."

She dropped the sheet, stood next to the bed, and began pulling on her clothing. In a few moments, she was gone. Zeb began tugging on his summer union suit.

"Bad trouble?" he asked.

"Very bad. The worst," I answered. "That lawman from Morgansville is in town asking questions."

"Damn," Stone cursed. "Was he alone?"

"I don't know. I saw him in Dalton's. He was alone then, questioning the clerk."

"That don't mean nothin'," Zeb said. "We'd best figure he's got some men with him. You got your horse, Pound?"

"Yes. Out in front."

"Damn," Stone repeated. "I sure ain't gonna face that man with my derringer. But if I strap on my iron over this suit, I'll stand out like a green cow in a snowbank." He chewed his lower lip for a moment. "Look: You go an' settle up at the stable an' get my horse saddled an' ready to go. I kept my ol' trail clothes. I'll put them on an' walk down after you. That way, my Colt won't look so strange. Soon's I get there, we'll pull for Silver Ridge."

"But suppose—"

"Move, Pound! Supposin' don't do nothin' but waste time we ain't got to waste!"

I mounted and rode at a walk to the stable at the south end of town. I had the eerie, crawly-skinned sensation that someone was watching me very, very closely. I wanted desperately to slam my heels against my horse's sides and feel him stretch out and cover ground. My throat was dry. The collar of my white shirt was saturated with sweat. My every nerve shrieked at me to run. I struggled with myself, but kept my horse at an unhurried walk.

When I dismounted in front of the stable, I gulped air like a man who has been saved from drowning. The stable hand inspected me curiously. I had to work some saliva into my mouth before I could speak.

"Saddle the roan," I said. "My friend will be right along." I handed a fifty-dollar bill to the man. "Does that cover the charges against the animal?" I asked.

The stable hand beamed at me. "Sure does—with more'n a little bit left over."

"Keep it," I said. "Just saddle the horse in a hurry."

He trotted down the row of stalls, bridle in hand. I sat on a hay bale outside the barn, my right hand in my suit coat pocket, grasping my derringer. I was sweating nervously, profusely, and the heavy animal reek of my perspiration told me just how frightened I was. The thought that less than an hour ago I was anticipating this type of action made me queasy, bringing me to the very verge of vomiting. I concentrated on Zeb, dressed in his trail clothes and with his Colt at his side, striding down the sidewalk toward the stable. He looked like a cowpuncher with absolutely nothing on his mind. He was, in fact, whistling. I stood and led my horse into the relative coolness of the barn. A couple of minutes later, Stone walked in.

"All set?" he asked.

"Your horse is being saddled, Zeb. I paid the bill.

We've got to get moving. That damned lawman . . ."

"Well, well," the voice from that obscenely maimed throat rasped, "it looks like I've found me a pair of kid-killers."

The sheriff was framed in the middle of the large, open front of the barn. Stone stepped to his left, away from me and my horse. Behind us the stable hand was jogging down the aisle, leading Zeb's saddled mount.

"Hey, what's goin'—" he began, and then saw Zeb and the lawman facing each other and dove into an empty stall, leaving the roan standing free. There was absolutely no mistaking the fact that a gunfight was about to take place.

Time seemed not to be quite stopped, but slowed to the degree where every motion, every sound, appeared unnatural and unreal.

Stone's boots were two feet apart, his left a few inches forward of his right. His upper body was angled slightly to his right, and his knees were bent as if he were about to drop into a crouch. The sheriff's words were the only sounds in the barn, and they were ponderous, heavy, as if he took a gulp of the hot, motionless air between each abrasive tone.

"I ain't takin' you alive, gunfighter."

Zeb neither moved nor answered. The fingers of his right hand were slowly curling inward, the most minute fraction of an inch at a time, toward the bone grips of his Colt.

"You're dead right now, boy," the lawman said. "I'm faster an' I'm better—an' you know that as well as I do. You an' your partner—you're both dead. I got one question I want answered before I gun you. How does a murderin', yellow-bellied—"

Time contradicted itself. Now everything was too fast; faster than a striking rattler, faster than lightning. The lawman's hand darted to his pistol with incredible, awesome speed. His weapon hadn't quite cleared leather when two slugs from Stone's Colt took him in the center of his chest. Amazingly, rather than going down, the sheriff took two disjointed, awkward steps backward. His pistol dropped to the ground next to him. His eyes were wide, incredulous, as if he couldn't believe he'd been outdrawn and mortally wounded. Stone raised his Colt and fired a third time. The slug tore through the lawman's heart. He fell flat on his back, arms spread wide on either side of him.

If I hadn't been standing so close to Zeb, I wouldn't have heard what he said in an almost inaudible whisper.

"You still faster an' better than I am, lawman? Are me an' Pound still dead?" Zeb spat contemptuously toward the body and said much louder, "Stupid trick, lawman. Stupid an' old. Maybe that question thing works on a Saturday-night drunk, but it don't work against no shootist."

I shook Stone's shoulder. "Come on, Zeb!" I shouted. "The whole damned town will be here in a minute!"

He looked at me blankly for a moment, almost as if he didn't recognize me. "Yeah," he said, shaking his head like a dog coming out of water. "Yeah."

Stone turned to walk back to his horse. At the

same instant, the stable hand peeked into the corridor from the stall in which he'd been hiding. I saw what was coming with terrible clarity.

"Zeb—no!" I yelled. "He's only the—"

Stone's gun hand was faster than my mouth. He put two bullets in the man's head. "Zeb," I yelled again, "he didn't have a gun! Come on—there's been enough killing here!"

My horse threw himself forward before I was completely in the saddle. I let his momentum pull me up, yanked him into a sharp left turn, and headed south at a full gallop. I heard the hoofbeats of Zeb's horse directly behind me.

Our horses were well fed, rested, and fresh. We stretched out the gallop as long as we dared. Stone urged his roan up next to me and made a downward motion with his hand. I checked my black to a lope and then to a walk. Stone did the same. I put my derringer in my right saddlebag and peeled off my suit coat and white shirt. I looked at Zeb.

"Might just as well drop 'em," he said. "We're leavin' a trail a blind man could follow anyways." I tossed the coat and shirt off to my side and then reined in and dismounted. Stone watched placidly as I dressed in the pants, shirt, boots, and hat I'd bought. The weight of my Smith & Wesson at my side had a decidedly calming effect on my nerves.

"Feels good, don't it, Pound?" Stone asked, nodding toward my pistol.

"Yeah," I said. "It feels good."

Stone, crazily, seemed inclined to sit there and talk as if we were at a church social. "A man ain't much without he's carryin' iron," he said conversationally. " 'Course, some men are better'n others when it comes to guns. Now, you take that lawman back there. Damn. The ol' fool didn't have a chance. See, what he was tryin' to do was get my mind offa business by askin' somethin' I'd have to think on. Then, see, he'd have the advantage. Another thing he done was to swing his eyes to the left real quick, hopin' my eyes would follow his while he up an' drew an' put some holes in me. Musta thought I was born yesterday."

"Zeb. . . ." It was obvious that Stone was in sort sort of shock. He ignored me.

"You'd best tie your holster down soon's you get a chance, pard," he said. "You come up against a real shootist—like me—an' you're gonna be feedin' grave worms if you have to fumble aroun' tryin' to haul out your iron."

"Zeb . . . please . . ."

"We ain't in a real good spot, Pound. We done in four people, includin' a kid an' a lawman. Folks don't take kindly to that."

"Five," I said. "Five."

"Five what?"

"We've killed five people, not four, Zeb."

"Bullshit."

"I can count, Zeb. Number five was the stable hand."

Zeb was silent, thinking, sorting things out in his mind. "There wasn't no stable hand," he said.

"I *watched* you kill him. How can you . . ."

Stone's eyes suddenly took on a deranged, feverish

151

glow. "There wasn't no stable hand," he said again.

"Right," I said, "no stable hand. But we have to move, partner. I imagine there's lots of people with lots of guns behind us, coming on fast."

"Yeah," Stone said. "Lots of people. But don't you fret none." He placed fresh cartridges in the empty chambers of his Colt with agonizing deliberation, as if he'd never done it before. "We've lost better posses than what's followin' us," he said.

"Zeb . . . please . . . let's ride. *Now*."

"Yeah," Stone answered. "Let's ride."

Never again in our time together did either of us mention Stone's killing of the stable hand.

But that didn't make the man any less dead.

Chapter Nine

My black and Zeb's roan were traveling strongly, easily, even though we were pushing them hard. The three weeks of prime grain and short periods of daily exercise had been precisely what the animals needed.

I kept a close watch over Zeb. His actions after the battle in the stable frightened me much more than I let on. It was obvious that he was somehow blocking the memory of gunning down the innocent stable hand. That, I suppose, I could understand. But the question that was gnawing at me concerned whether or not I could trust Zeb to make the correct—the best—decisions when our lives literally depended on his judgment.

I couldn't get out of my mind the image of the sheriff taking the third round Stone fired at him. There was the air of an execution about that shot: For some reason, I saw Stone's first two rounds as self-defense. The third, however, was calculated and coldhearted. It's not that the sheriff could have lived before the third shot was fired. I'm positive the first two rounds did enough damage to kill the man twice over. Rather, it was the manner in which it was delivered. Stone's Colt had been partially lowered. He raised it slowly, thumbed back the hammer, hesitated another half second, and fired. That bullet had missed the sheriff's star by perhaps a quarter of an inch—it was that precisely aimed and delivered. I didn't like the thoughts I was having about Zeb. He'd killed the sheriff as much for *me* as he had for himself. And if Zeb hadn't been a shootist, we'd both be sitting in a cell waiting to meet an executioner.

It occurred to me that Zeb Stone had changed as much as I myself had in the short period of time we'd been outlawing together. Zeb had told me in the saloon in Burnt Rock that he'd never killed anyone. Now four men were in graves because of his bone-gripped Colt—and I'd have been a fool to think that others weren't fated to join them.

I wondered how long it would be before I pulled the trigger on a man. After all, I'd already put two bullets into a child. I wondered if I'd be able to kill again if it became necessary to protect Zeb or myself. I shuddered a bit as the answer came to me: I'd do it. With little hesitation, I'd do it. I wouldn't like it, nor would I like myself after doing it, but I knew that I'd kill if it became the only way to keep us alive and free.

We didn't rest our mounts for more than a few minutes at a time until it was fully dark. We reined in at a small water hole, let the horses suck, and loosened our cinches. We both drank our fill. Stone checked hooves and felt under the saddles to make sure that the blankets were molded to the horse's backs, without wrinkles. There was a full moon, but clouds scudded across it often, making visibility unsure. Even in the dark, I was able to see that Zeb's eyes had lost that psychopathic fire I'd noticed earlier. I experienced a twinge of guilt concerning my earlier thoughts of Stone's competence.

Zeb shook tobacco from a Bull Durham sack onto a leaf of paper and then stopped, midmotion, as he raised the rolled cigarette to his mouth to lick and seal the edge.

"Damn," he said.

"What's the matter?" I asked.

"Listen close, Pound. Hold your breath in an' listen as tight as you can."

I closed my eyes and held my breath. In a few moments, I heard it: the faraway drumming of hoofbeats coming our way.

"Damn fools gotta be crazy ridin' that hard on a night like this," Zeb said. "Too many clouds blockin' the moonlight. Listen to 'em come! They must want us real bad."

"What do we do?"

"Ride faster'n them loons, an' hope we get some kind of a break along the way."

"Like what? What kind of break?"

"How the hell do I know? We ain't got but two choices: stay here an' get all shot to hell, or ride towards Silver Ridge, hopin' somethin' turns in our favor." He listened for a moment longer. "Right now," he said quietly, "we ain't in real good shape as far as seein' old age goes."

We pulled our cinches, mounted, and set out from the water hole at a gallop. It was impossible to see the ground in front of us. Most of the time, the night was one of a thick, murky darkness that failed to allow the nebulous definition of the terrain that even mere shadows would cast. The wind became gusty at our backs, prodding us ahead with the sounds of the horses and men behind us. We were riding at a lunatic pace over ground we not only didn't know but couldn't even see. A man can trust his luck only so far, and then the odds run out on him.

We rode side by side, Zeb to my left, our horses stretched, digging for traction, their heads almost parallel with the ground. My black's left shoulder suddenly dropped far downward, and almost simultaneously there was a blacksnake-whip type of crack and a shuddering scream of agony from him as he went down. He careened into the right side of Zeb's horse, and then all was flying dirt and flailing steel horseshoes, and, for me, a fall down a vividly, excruciatingly bright well. I caught the glint of moonlight on the shoe before it hit me just above my right ear. I'm not even sure if it was Zeb's horse's or mine, and it didn't make a damned bit of difference either way.

Bright scraps of scenes flitted through my brain for the shortest part of a second, and then all was dark.

"This one dead?" I felt a callused thumb press roughly at the pulse point under my jaw.

"Naw, he ain't dead," a different voice responded. "But, God—lookit the knob on his head. An' that cut runs right clean into his skull all along this side. Looks like somebody was tryin' to scalp him. I seen the body of a man what got scalped during the Sioux troubles, an' this is just how he looked."

I kept my eyes closed. The keening of a horse was mercifully ended with the flat boom of a shotgun.

"Get a fire going here," a deep voice commanded. "You boys'll have plenty of time to gawk at these pieces of trash. Drag the one with the busted head over here." A pair of hands grasped me under my arms and yanked my head and chest from the ground. I think I screamed. I know I blacked out.

I could hear words, curses, boots on sand, and the jingle of spurs, yet I wasn't completely conscious. I thought I heard Zeb's voice, but I'm not sure about that. The owner of the deep voice that had ordered a fire built seemed to be in charge. Or, at least, he seemed to be giving the orders.

The trembling of my body from the moist, cool, night air awakened me. I opened my eyes. A yard from my head a man was sitting, wrapped in a blanket, a rifle across his lap. Although I was within the circle of light of a fire, next to no heat reached me. I moved slightly, and the barrel of the rifle swung toward my chest.

"Trent," the man with the rifle said, "this here baby killer's awake."

Boots crunched over the sandy soil toward me. The deep voice I'd heard earlier came from above me. "You're one lucky killer, Taylor. My name's Trent. I'm a Texas Ranger. If I wasn't, these boys woulda torn you and Stone apart. I still have half a mind to turn my back and let 'em at you. But I took me an oath, and I'll get you to a jail. It don't make much sense, but I'll do it. If you don't croak on the way, you'll stretch a rope. Same goes for Stone." He spat next to my head. "Neither one of you deserves to draw breath."

The Ranger hunkered down next to me. "You two snakes can do me a big favor," he said. "Try to escape. I'd like that a whole lot." He stood and called to one of the men near the fire. "Lou—tie this one like the other. Tight—real tight. We don't want these kid-killers runnin' off on us." The contempt—the hatred—in the Ranger's voice made me cringe like a dog under the whip. Someone dragged me closer to the fire. I lost consciousness again.

It was barely dawn when I awoke. I was trussed so tightly that I had no sensation in my hands or feet. My head hurt me more than I'd ever been hurt before. Hangover headaches were nothing compared to this. Zeb was a couple of yards from me, tied in the same fashion. The weak light from the dying fire cast a glow on the upper part of his body and his head. His eyes were closed. I assumed he was asleep. His face was livid with purplish-yellow bruises, and there was a large spread of dried blood on his beard and the front of his shirt. His forehead glistened with sweat, although I was so cold my teeth began to chatter. Stone's mouth was partly open. His lower front teeth were gone and his lips were lacerated and swollen. As I stared at him, his eyes popped open and met with mine. Then, as impossible as it sounds, he winked at me and tried a grin, which began his lips bleeding anew. I closed my eyes.

God, I thought, he really *is* crazy. He actually

thinks we're going to get out of this. He's plain, flat-out insane, and I'm going to hang from the end of a rope because I listened to him in an insignificant lit-tle town called Burnt Rock, Texas, what seemed like a long, long tme ago.

The posse member stretched out closest to me woke, stood, yawned, and walked off to relieve himself. Immediately, a silver-haired, sleepy-eyed man of about sixty squatted down in front of me. A knife slid butt-first into his hand from under his sleeve.

I'm not going to hang at all, I thought. This fellow is going to cut my throat.

The knife must have been extremely sharp. The ropes on my wrists and ankles offered light resis-tance to the blade. The old gentleman slipped a pis-tol into my shirt. "Don't make a move 'til Zeb does," he whispered. He stood and walked back closer to the remains of the fire. The pain of the blood return-ing to my hands and feet was almost—but not quite—as bad as what was going on in my head. I stayed perfectly still, watching Zeb through slitted eyes. Other members of the posse began to stir. Be-hind me I could hear a horse cropping at buffalo grass. The clink of a horseshoe against a pebble sounded quite loud. A nightbird of some kind trilled and then was silent.

Then all hell broke loose.

Zeb was crouched, levering shots out of a Win-chester carbine. The Ranger was on his feet and swinging his pistol toward Stone. Zeb put a bullet through the badge over the man's heart, rolled and crouched again, and dropped a man who was lifting a sawed-off shotgun. Before I realized what I was doing, I found myself on my knees, shooting at anything that moved except Zeb. The old man was behind me, firing a Sharps. The thunder of the buffalo rifle made the reports of the other weapons sound puny and without power. The early-morning air was thick with the acrid stink of gunpowder.

"Drop your guns!" Stone shouted. "Hands up—we don't want to kill you all! Drop the guns!"

The gunfire ended as abruptly as it had begun. Six of the posse were dead or dying. Seven others, some with minor wounds, stood near the coals of the fire, hands raised above their heads. Zeb pushed himself up from his crouch and stood, the still-smoking barrel of the Winchester pointing at the ground. The old man handed the Sharps to me and said, "Watch 'em close, boy. Anybody moves, you put a hole through him. Careful of the kick on that there rifle—it'll drop you if you ain't ready for it."

Simultaneously, Zeb and the old man whooped like a pair of liquored-up Indians and ran toward each other. They met with a bone-breaking collison that would have downed lesser men. Zeb whacked the old man on the back with his fists, yelling, laughing, and spewing blood from his mouth onto himself and his friend. The elderly gent put a bear hug on Zeb that could have caved in the sides of a beer barrel. They pushed apart and stood at arm's length from each other, still laughing.

"Sweetwater Eddie," Stone shouted, "damn me if I

didn't think you was dead an' buried behind some cathouse!"

"I'll live to spit on *your* grave, you young pup!" Sweetwater Eddie bellowed.

Arms over each other's shoulders, they walked to me, stepping over and around sprawled bodies.

"Pound," Zeb said, "I want you to shake hands with this ol' rattlesnake. He just evened up a debt he's owed me for a couple of years an' better." I tossed the Sharps to Zeb and shook hands with Sweetwater Eddie. His grip was firm and dry. There was enough light to see that he was dressed in a fringed leather jacket, denim pants, high black boots, and a fine-looking black Stetson. His silver-white hair hung well below his shoulders, and his eyes were as deep a blue as any I've ever seen.

"We owe you, sir," I said.

"Cut the 'sir,' boy. Just call me Sweet. An' you don't owe me nothin'. Like Zeb said, I was payin' off a old debt. Stone there, he saved me from bein' strung up a couple years back. Testified right in court, he did. Swore me an' him was playin' cards at the time a jealous huband got himself gunned down.

"Were you? Playing cards, I mean."

"Hell, no." Sweet laughed. "The husband, a man as dumb as a post for true, busted into his bedroom just as I'd finished pleasurin' his wife. Had him a little hideout gun, he did. Put a slug into his wife while I was scramblin' around lookin' for my iron. I found it and dropped him dead. Problem is, a drover testified he seen me runnin' buck nekkid out the back door of the house, carryin' my clothes, boots, and iron."

"What about the wife?" I asked.

Sweet smiled dreamily. "She was nothin' short of tremendous, boy."

"I meant, did she testify?"

"Nope. She croaked that afternoon. See, it was Zeb's word against the drover's. Folks, they went along with Zeb. 'Course, they knew if they strung me up, Zeb'd still be around. That's what turned the tide."

"Oh," I said. "Oh."

"Sweet," Stone asked, looking over the remnants of the posse, "how'd you come to be ridin' with a damned Ranger?"

Sweet chuckled richly. "Plain good luck, is what I call it. I was just down the street when I heard shots an' seen that fella with the big scar on his throat flop down in the doorway of the stable. Then you an' your pard come out spurrin' to beat hell an' I knowed there was trouble." He punched Zeb on the shoulder. "Almost didn't pick you out with that beard. Anyways, when the Ranger—Trent—started deputizin' men, I figured I'd do you boys more good in the posse than I would ridin' with you. Say—you didn't gun no kid like they was sayin', did you? I said to myself, 'Sweet, ol' Zeb Stone wouldn't shoot no kid, an' he wouldn't ride with a man who would.' That's exactly what I said to myself."

"Well," Zeb admitted, "a boy did get shot. Thing is, it was a accident. Couldn't be helped. We was robbin' a stage. I'll tell you this, though, Sweet: Pound here wouldn't shoot a kid for all the money in Texas. He just ain't that kind of man."

"Oh," Sweet said. "I guess you can't do nothin' 'bout accidents. They happen in all lines of work, I guess." He looked around at the carnage from the gunfight. "I come to Houston to play some cards an' drink some whiskey, an' here I am with a pair of gen-you-wine outlaws. I hear there's good money out on both of you. Hell, I might gun you myself an' fetch you in for the reward," he said, and grinned.

Stone smiled, blood still running down his chin. " 'Member that time you an' me got Chicken Barwell drunk an' tried to turn him in to the law as Billy the Kid for the reward money?"

" 'Course I remember." Sweetwater Eddie laughed. "Only the marshal didn't believe us, an' then Chicken, he upchucked on the man's desk."

"How much is on our heads?" I asked.

"Lessee," Sweet answered. "Moore Coach Lines put a thousand apiece on you, an' the law boosted that by five hundred a head."

Zeb attempted to spit, forgetting he had no lower front teeth. Saliva and blood dribbled down his chin and onto his shirt. "Fifteen hundred?? That's all? Hell, me an' Pound are worth a sight more'n that. It's a damn insult."

"Well, but the law will up the ante now that the Ranger got his lights put out," Sweet said. "You're right, though. Fifteen hundred *is* a bit light."

"It just don't seem fair," Zeb said. "Sweet—will you hold your Sharps on these boys so's me an' Pound can tie them up?"

"Glad to," Sweet answered. "But there's a easier way to keep them quiet so's they don't just ride back to Houston an' come after us all over again. Hell, ammo's cheap, Zeb."

Zeb turned to face his old friend. The smile was gone from his face. "We're gonna tie 'em, Sweet. That's the way it's gonna be."

"Don't mean much to me either way," Sweet said. "I just thought it might make sense an' save us some time. But you boys go ahead an' tie them just like you said."

The seven men no longer looked like a posse. There was fear in their eyes—fear that was all the more desperate because their leader had been cut down. They reminded me of a group of schoolboys caught stealing candy from a general store. Without their weapons and Trent to lead them, they were sheep. I could literally smell the feral reek of fear on them as Stone and I began tying them just as they'd tied us.

"Nice an' tight," Zeb said. "I want 'em to soak up some sun before they get loose."

I did as I was instructed, pulling the sections of rope cut with Sweetwater Eddie's knife as tightly as I could, doubling each knot. I'd just finished trussing one of the men when black spots began to flit and dance before my eyes and I heard a loud buzzing sound in both my ears. I dropped to one knee and then fell to my side. Then everything that had remained in my stomach rose in my throat and spewed out of my mouth in an acidic, vile-smelling rush. I coughed a couple of times before I passed out, which may have saved my life. I'd heard of men drowning in their own vomit. That could have quite easily happened to me if I hadn't retained consciousness as long as I did. The buzzing grew in volume and in intensity, until it seemed like every angry wasp and hornet in the world was trapped in my head. There wasn't any room for thought in my mind: The insect racket took every iota of space in my brain, building to a shriek that was ended only when I passed out.

I felt gentle, probing fingers at the wound on my head. "Might have one of them concussions," Sweet said. "Maybe not, though. I can't really tell. See, the cut ain't clean—there's a slew of pus an' muck in it. If it festers, your pard will croak, sure's you're born, Zeb. Head wounds will put a man in the ground damn near as fast as a lung shot from a .45 will. I seen it at Harpers Ferry an' at Antioch, too. A man'd take a whack from a rifle butt an' not think too much of it, an' then he'd start pukin', an' the next thing you knowed, he was dead."

"Can we clean Pound's head?" Zeb asked.

"Got to," Sweet answered. "Ain't no choice involved. Pound ain't gonna be too happy about it, though. But, like I said, we ain't got a choice. You'll have to hold him, Zeb. I'll go through the saddlebags an' see if I can't find some whiskey. You got them boys all tied up?"

"Yeah," Zeb answered. "Don't bother with the whiskey. Pound swore off it. He wouldn't drink it even if you found it."

"Ain't to drink. I want to use it to help clean the cut with. Cheap booze is almost as good as that medicinal alcohol the sawbones used durin' the war."

I drifted in and out of consciousness. I heard Sweet walking back to us. "Let's do her," he said.

"Yeah," Zeb agreed. "Let's do her." He knelt next to me and then shifted himself so he was sitting on my chest with a knee on each shoulder. He turned my head so the wounded side was up.

"Ready?" Sweet asked.

"Ready as we'll ever be, I guess," Zeb answered. I didn't like the tone of his voice. He sounded very frightened.

I was lucky. I passed out within a half a minute or so after Sweet poured whiskey into the wound and began picking out dirt, dried and crusted blood, and matted hair. I was blessedly unconscious when Sweet did his best to sew the ragged edges of the laceration together, using fishing line and a veterinary needle he always carried in his gear. Zeb told me about that afterward. He said he was glad I was out, and that the procedure wasn't a pretty one.

Stone shook my shoulder gently. I opened my eyes. My head was ablaze with pain. Sweet put a canteen to my mouth and I drank deeply. It didn't do much good. My mouth and throat remained parched and the residue of my vomit tasted metallic and poisonous. I looked around. The sun was nearing midday.

"Can you ride, Pound?" Zeb asked. He knew as well as I did that there was no option or choice involved. I *had* to sit a horse. Tying me over the back of a horse would probably have killed me.

"I can ride," I said. I got my feet under me and stood. I was swaying like a tall, aged tree in a windstorm, but I was standing on my own. The buzzing in my ears had abated slightly, but it came rushing back with renewed power as soon as I was on my feet.

While I'd slept, Zeb had selected the two best horses from those owned by the members of the posse. The rest he'd run off. He'd chosen a tough, trail-wise-looking bay mare for me and a tall, broad-chested Appaloosa for himself. He told me his roan had snapped a pastern in the collision with my horse and the posse had finished off both animals. He said my black's left front leg was broken both high and low. I hoped he'd died quickly; he was a damned good horse.

Sweetwater Eddie rode a one-eyed black gelding he said he'd raised from a foal. He said the horse never had two working eyes, so he got along just fine with only one. Actually, the horse *had* two eyes, but the right one was a dull, flat gray in color and didn't move when the left eye did.

Sweet and Zeb had collected all the weapons and ammunition carried by the posse, and all their canteens, as well. We had six rifles, nine pistols, two shotguns, and a long-bladed Bowie knife. As Sweet wrapped the weapons in his oilcloth rain slicker, Zeb led me away from the captives.

"Sweet's throwin' in with us," he said. "We'll do Silver Ridge an' Paris, just like we decided."

I nodded.

"But here's the thing, Pound: Sweet says you need a few days' rest for your concussion to heal good.

He's got himself a safe place acrost the Colorado an' down south ten or twelve miles. The river's less'n twenty miles from here. He says it's a cave an' that you can't see it 'lessen you're lookin' for it an' know where it's at. I figure we can lay up there for two or three days while your melon heals. Ain't nobody goin' to find us there. See, we can ride most of the way in the river an' not leave no tracks."

"Okay. What about the posse?"

"Well . . . Sweet, he wants to kill them."

"God, Zeb! Seven helpless shopkeepers and clerks! I won't—"

"Yeah, yeah, I know," Stone said. "I talked him out of it." He looked into my eyes for a long moment. "I got to tell you somethin' about Sweet. See, at times he gets as loony as a bedbug. He's got hidin' places all over Texas, most of which he's forgot where they're at. The law's got paper on him, too."

"What for?"

Stone looked away from me. "Well, he got in a argument at one of them religion tent shows, an' he . . . well, he . . ."

"He *what?*"

"Well. Damn, Pound. He . . . uhh . . . what he done was, he gunned down the preacher an' two fellas dressed in white robes an' put a couple shots into some ladies singin' in the choir. But hell, Pound, that don't mean nothin'. Ain't nobody perfect. The man *saved* us. That Ranger could have recognized him, or he could've got plugged in the battle here. But he stuck with us an' sewed up your head real good, an' he's takin' us to a safe place. 'Cept for bein' screwy, he's a pretty fair partner. He kinda changes his mind about things sometimes, but everybody does that."

"Wonderful," I said. "Wonderful."

Zeb looped my reins around my saddle horn. I held the horn with both hands, slumped my shoulders, and let my chin rest on my chest. Sweet rode on my left and Zeb on my right, leading my mare with a short piece of rope, keeping her between the other two horses. When I began to tilt one way or the other, Zeb or Sweet would grab my shoulder and hold me in my saddle until the dizziness passed. We rode at a fast walk. Early on, we'd tried a lope. If Zeb hadn't caught me, I'd have toppled from my saddle.

Every so often, Zeb held a canteen to my mouth and I drank what I could. The pain in my head was terrible. I cracked a piece off a back tooth clenching and grinding my jaws because of it. Sweet gave me a thick, barklike piece of venison jerky to clamp onto—like biting a bullet, I suppose. We rode all day. There was little conversation. Or, perhaps, I heard only small bits of what was said. I do know that I didn't like some of the things that I heard. Even through the pain and the buzzing in my ears and the fever I was running, I was deeply disturbed.

"We shoulda gunned that posse, Zeb," Sweet said at one point. "I ain't yet heard of a dead man who could give directions or information. We shoulda shot 'em dead—the whole damned bunch of 'em. You think any of them woulda thunk twice about killin' us? Hell no!"

"We already talked that into the ground," Zeb answered. "First of all, nobody's gonna miss the posse.

Everybody will figure they're still doggin' us. Who the hell goes out to search for a posse, Sweet? An' it'll take them men a good long time to get untied. They don't know where we're goin', an' we'll be layin' up in your cave by the time they walk back to Houston. Wasn't no reason to gun 'em."

"Scripture says a man should pluck the eye outta anybody who offends him. Or kill 'em—either way is okay, accordin' to the Good Book," Sweet growled.

A couple of hours of silence followed that conversation. Then Sweetwater Eddie spoke again.

"We ain't makin' no time, Stone. Hell, a ol' lady on foot would slide right past an' leave us in her dust."

"Pound can't ride no faster," Zeb answered.

"Yeah, but we can—you an' me."

Stone cleared his throat. "He's my pard," he said.

"I don't care who he is! I ain't about to swing on his account."

Zeb spoke slowly and carefully. "Then ride, Sweet. You an' me don't owe each other nothin' now. We're even. Nobody's holdin' a gun on you. Ride on alone or shut the hell up. I don't leave no pard for the buzzards."

Sweet grunted disgustedly but kept silent after that, except for some mumbling that sounded like a bizarre cross between prayer and cursing.

Chapter Ten

I recall the day giving way to dusk, and then to night. I drifted in and out of a hazy state of semi-sleep, constantly plagued by the screeching buzz in my ears, and alternating between sweating and the cold shakes. We crossed the Colorado when it was, once again, day. We'd ridden all night, although I have very little recollection of that period of time. The steady chunk-clink of shod hooves striking ground was transformed to a sloppy, inharmonious splashing sound as the horses pushed through hock-high water. We rode against the current, in water deep enough so that any tracks would be obliterated by the force of the river.

"Pound surely does stink," Sweet said disgustedly. "Look—the damned fool went an' wet his drawers."

There was anger in Stone's voice. "You'd wet your pants, too, if you'd got your head near kicked off like Pound did."

The sharp, stinging cold of the river filling my boots and slapping against my legs helped to dissipate some of the mist in my mind. "How much farther?" I asked.

Sweet answered before Zeb had a chance to speak. "A dozen or so miles," he said. "Be about a hour's ride if we wasn't haulin' a ton of deadwood with us."

Zeb nudged his horse a bit closer to Sweetwater Eddie. When Stone spoke there was a coldness in his voice I couldn't remember hearing before. "Lookit here, Sweet," he said. "First of all, Pound ain't deadwood. He's my partner. An' second, you got a bug up your ass about somethin' an' you're raggin' on ol' Pound for no good reason. I'm tellin' you to stop it."

"You're *telling* me? Where the hell do you get off—"

"Don't push this, Sweet," Zeb said almost too quietly for me to hear.

The silence between the three of us felt not unlike the moment before a lightning strike. I didn't like it even a little bit and was trying to dredge up something conciliatory when Sweet chuckled.

"Damn if you ain't still a ball of fire, Zeb," he said. "This ain't been my best day, is all. No sense in none of us getting' up on our back feet, is there?"

"Nope," Zeb said. "There ain't."

Sweet's place was a good one. It was a cave with a relatively small mouth that was covered with tangles of vine and rampant scrub and some sort of thick bushes. I couldn't see the entrance from ten feet away, and Stone had difficulty picking it out, as well. "See?" Sweet said proudly. "My personal saviour, He fixed up this little spot on earth jus' for me—an' my friends, 'course."

The cave was deep and cool and the air inside

smelled slightly musty, a bit like rotting vegetation, but not at all unpleasant. I was seeing spots floating before my eyes again and was glad the long and tedious ride was over.

Zeb dragged some light branches and leaves to the rear of the hideout and helped me to stretch out on the makeshift bed. I drank some water and fell into an almost comatose, dreamless sleep.

Sweetwater Eddie did nothing at all to change my disquieting thoughts about him. From that long ride forward, he rarely spoke directly to me. Rather, he'd make comments to Zeb within my hearing, and it was up to me to respond or not as I saw fit. Through the first day in the cave, Zeb became increasingly nervous, feeling—and justifiably so—that he'd somehow gotten into the middle of a battle he didn't understand. For that matter, *I* didn't understand it, either.

"Zeb," Sweet said that evening, "when's Pound gonna be able to ride? I get jumpy-like bein' in one place too long. It ain't no good for my eternal soul—an' it ain't no good for yours, either."

"We just got here, Sweet," Zeb answered. "Pound'll ride soon's he can—no sooner'n no later." The tone of voice Stone used was strange: He sounded like he was explaining a difficult concept to a slow-learning child.

Sweet grunted, got to his feet, grabbed up his Sharps, and stomped out of the cave. Zeb looked at me, and our eyes held for a long moment before we both looked away.

I slid in and out of a restless sleep, and when I

awoke I felt limp and weak. I was either burning with fever or so cold my dreams were of Texas winters, with howling winds and cattle freezing to death where they stood and spittle freezing solid between the time it left a man's mouth and when it hit the ground.

I awoke the second morning to find Sweet kneeling on the cave floor a couple of feet from me. His hands were folded in prayer, and the tears running from both his eyes and down his cheeks glistened in the light of the fire. His gaze was focused somewhere above and beyond me, and his eyes had a strange flat-gray cast to them. He seemed to be reciting some sort of litany, although I couldn't hear well enough to distinguish actual words. He rocked back and forth several inches in a rhythm with whatever it was he was saying.

My throat was as dry as desert alkali and my lips were cracked to the point of bleeding. I wanted—needed—a drink of water just then far more powerfully than I'd ever wanted or needed a drink of whiskey. I was barely able to force sound out of my throat, and so weak even moving my head was almost impossible. Zeb wasn't around, or I would never have asked Sweet what I did.

"Sweet," I rasped, "please . . . some water."

The flatness left his eyes in an instant and was replaced by a malevolent liquid blackness that was as frighteningly evil as the death stare of a rattlesnake intent on striking.

"I will bring no water to a whore of Babylon," he said clearly and distinctly.

I closed my eyes to get away from him, and kept them closed until Zeb strolled in, buttoning his pants. He stopped, looking from Sweet to me and then back to Sweet. "What's goin' on here?" he asked.

"I was prayin' over Pound. I guess maybe I woke him up."

Zeb picked up a canteen and walked over to me. "Seems like some water might do ol' Pound more good than prayers right now," he said. He pulled the cork out of the canteen and held it to my mouth. Sweet watched for a moment and then turned and left us alone.

I drank the canteen dry. "He's crazy, Zeb," I said urgently. "And he's getting crazier by the minute. He's going to kill me. He's got some kind of idea that I'm an evil spirit or something. We've got to . . ."

Zeb chuckled. "His prayers ain't gonna croak you, Pound. That's just Sweet's way, is all. Hell, why kill you now after he up an' saved your life? It don't make no sense."

"He wasn't crazy when he saved my life, Zeb! Something has snapped in his mind!" My throat felt more raw with each word, but I ignored the pain. "He's going to kill me—and he'll probably kill you, too."

"You gotta rest up, Pound," Zeb said. "Seems like your fever's givin' you crazy dreams like a fever'll do."

"That's not it," I insisted. "You haven't heard—"

"Now dammit, Pound, Sweet's been my friend for a lotta years. Sure, he's screwy. But he ain't so screwy that he's gonna kill a partner of mine." His voice became more sharp as he spoke. "I know the man an' you don't, an' you ain't thinkin' straight 'cause of your head bein' busted open. You just get rested up an' everything'll be fine. Forget about Sweet—he don't mean you no harm."

Zeb turned away before I could answer. I sank back on my bed of leaves. A thought struck me as I was sliding back into sleep. Zeb had, I realized suddenly, known Sweetwater Eddie for one hell of a lot longer than he'd known me. Would it be possible that Zeb would side with Sweet against me? Could he be swayed so much by his old friend that he'd allow Sweet to kill me?

My recovery was a slow and painful process. The intense headaches that throbbed in cadence with my pulse continued, although they became shorter in duration as the days passed. The buzzing in my ears was abating slowly, but I was having problems with dizziness—with spots floating before my eyes.

I woke one night to find the weapons we'd collected from the posse spread out on an oilskin slicker next to me, where they'd be out of the way. The metallic scent of gun oil hung in the air: Either Sweet or Zeb had cleaned and oiled the firearms.

The sent of cooking rabbit tugged me awake the morning of the fifth day we spent in the cave. I had to rub my gummed-shut, gritty eyes to get them open, and I felt kitten weak. But the fever had broken. For the first time since the incident, I woke without my shirt pasted to my chest by sweat.

"Zeb," I whispered hoarsely. In a second he was on his knees next to me.

PARTNERS

"Water?" he asked. I nodded.

I drank a full canteen of icy cold Colorado River water and found myself suddenly tremendously hungry. Zeb brought me several pieces of rabbit, which I couldn't get down fast enough to suit me.

"Well," Stone beamed, "if it ain't ol' Pound. You're lookin' one hell of a lot better. I was wonderin' for a bit whether you was goin' to make it."

"So was I," I said. "So was I."

"You just keep on drinkin' an' eatin', an' you'll be fit to ride in no time."

"Where's Sweet?" I asked.

Zeb's smile disappeared as if it had been slapped from his face. "I ain't sure—out prayin' somewheres, I guess. You was right, Pound. He's turned crazy. I disremember seein' him this bad before. He's been talkin' evil spirit stuff about you, just like you said." Stone turned to look at the front of the cave and then went on.

"He don't look right. You know how them Mex cowboys look when they've been smokin' their hemp? That's the way Sweet looks, with his eyes all crazy an' wild. I figured maybe he'd snap outta it, but he's gettin' worse 'stead of better. He don't make no sense when he talks. I ain't left him alone with you in two days. I was scared he'd make a offer to heaven outta you. I can't figure what set him off—he started talkin' crazy soon's we rode away from where we got took by Trent." He shook his head sadly. "Damn, Pound, my ol' friend Sweet has up an' gone pure loony—"

"Zebulon Stone!" Sweetwater Eddie's voice

177

boomed from the very front of the cave. "Why do you lie about me to this foul spirit?"

Stone was hunkered down facing me, his back to the front of the cave. He began to stand.

"Stay where you are!" Sweet hollered. Zeb shifted a bit to get his feet under him, but didn't move otherwise.

Over Zeb's left shoulder I could see Sweet framed in the cave opening, a semitransparent drape of vines and foliage behind him. His Sharps was in his right hand, barrel pointed at the ground. In his left hand he held a cross fashioned from a pair of finger-thick saplings. We could hear every breath Sweet took. He was gasping for air as if he'd run for miles. Zeb was right about his eyes: They were a pair of embers sunken into his pale, stubble-shaded face. He'd drawn a cross on his forehead with mud, and it was being washed away—eroded—by his sweat.

"You sinners knoweth not the way to Glory," he bellowed. "But I damned well do! My earthly father wore the robes and preached the word, and so will I. I'll follow in his sweet footsteps an' slay whatever needs dyin', be it man or beast or spirit!"

There was an Army colt within a foot of my left hand. The weapons were arranged neatly on the slicker, rifles and shotguns at the top with their actions jacked open, and the pistols below them. I could probably reach the Colt without Sweet seeing me, thanks to Zeb's position. There were two problems: I didn't know if the pistol was loaded, and I'd never fired a weapon with my left hand.

Sweet held his cross out to us at arm's length. I saw

the barrel of the Sharps quiver. He could take us both with one shot from the buffalo rifle. Stone's back wouldn't even slow the slug, and my chest probably wouldn't, either. The now-familiar black spots began to drift about in my vision, growing, multiplying. I had very little time.

Was the damned Colt loaded?

I didn't dare move—nor to even whisper to Zeb. It was obvious it wouldn't take much to push Sweet into firing. There were more spots. The barrel of the Sharps twitched. If I didn't do something, Zeb and I were going to end our lives at the hands of a madman who'd saved us before killing us. I squinted, trying to push away the spots. It had no effect. I could feel cold sweat on my forehead and dampness in my palms. Sweet began to raise the barrel of his rifle.

"Down, Zeb!" I shouted, grabbing up the Colt. Stone dove to his left as I jerked the pistol from the slicker. I began pulling the trigger well before the muzzle was leveled at Sweet. The dirt wall took three bullets, and Sweet's chest and upper body got the other three. The velocity of the slugs flung Sweet backward through the foliage, as if he were a doll thrown by a cranky child. The noise in the cave was almost too much for the ear to bear. After my first shot, I heard nothing but a clamorous din of high-pitched ringing. I choked on the clouds of burnt gunpowder, and my eyes ran with tears from the haze. Stone was up and past me, Colt in hand, before I dropped my weapon. I settled back and did my best to regulate my breathing.

Stone returned to the cave in an hour. The ringing

in my head was greatly diminished. I was both hungry and thirsty. I was also concerned about what I could say to Zeb.

"Dead?" I asked stupidly, already knowing the answer.

"Dead?" Zeb repeated. "Yeah, I hope to tell you he's dead. You put three hunks of lead in him—there's no way he could be alive." Our eyes met. "You done real good, Pound—you done the only thing you could. I couldn't have drawed an' got turned around to shoot before Sweet put out our lights."

Stone sat down next to the coals of the fire. "I dragged ol' Sweet down the river a piece an' wedged him between two boulders real good, an' then I piled a bunch of rocks on top, coverin' him all up. He ain't goin' nowhere 'til the spring floods."

"I don't know how to say this, Zeb. I know Sweet was your—"

"You got no need to say nothin'," Zeb said. "That wasn't my friend you gunned. It was a crazy man who'da killed us both if you gave him a few more seconds. But damn, Pound: What set him off? He was sayin' you was slowin' us down, holdin' us back, but he could have rode on alone anytime he wanted. It don't make sense. Here he saves our hides an' then wants to blow holes in us with a damn buffalo rifle. It don't figure, Pound. It just don't."

Zeb rolled a pair of cigarettes, lit them both, and handed one to me. We smoked in silence.

"Why," Stone asked abruptly, "would Sweet want to up an' do somethin' like killin' us?"

"I don't know, Zeb," I answered. "I don't know."

"Maybe you repeatin' most everything you say twice drove him nuts," Zeb snickered. "Hell, sometimes *I* felt like gunnin' you."

I tossed the nub of my smoke into the dead coals of the fire and closed my eyes without bothering to answer.

"Sweet, he got real bad headaches before he went screwy when I rode with him," Zeb said. "Could be he got one right after the fight with the posse an' didn't let on. The thing is, a sore head don't give the man the right to kill his friends." Stone smiled proudly, as if he'd just said something quite profound. "I'll tell you what, Pound: I'll go out an' get us some rabbits or whatever else I come acrost an' we'll have us a big meal. How's that sound?"

I waved my hand at him, indicating I didn't much care what he did as long as he left me alone for a bit. His arguments—his addlepated logic—often had that effect on me. Zeb left the cave, humming to himself.

I was on the edge of sleep when what I'd done finally registered its full impact on me. I sat bolt upright, staring toward the front of the cave where Sweet had stood. I'd just killed a man by putting three bullets in his body, I thought. One second he'd been alive, heart beating, lungs drawing breath, and the next he was dead—a lump of meat useless to anyone or anything but carrion eaters.

The face of the little boy on the stage forced its way into my mind, and I again saw the lawman in Houston with that foolishly astounded, unbelieving look on his face as he died. I saw the flash of Zeb's Colt and the two holes appear in the stable hand's forehead. I relived the battle with the posse a few days ago: All the killing sickened me, made me wonder just what I'd become. Sweetwater Eddie had been insane and extremely dangerous. Perhaps that situation had been one of self-defense—kill or be killed. But, I wondered, why did I empty the pistol into him and keep on pulling the trigger until the hammer had clicked impotently several times on empty cartridges? Was it necessary for me to *kill* Sweet to save Stone's and my own life? Wouldn't one slug have dropped him, incapacitated him? The man had doctored my head and quite probably saved my life. And yet I'd snuffed his life with the same amount of thought Zeb gave to the ugly mutt he'd killed in Morgansville. What in the name of God was I becoming—what had I already become?

I picked up the Colt from where I'd dropped it and threw it as hard as I could toward the front of the cave. My aim was poor. The pistol skidded along the dirt wall, struck a piece of exposed root, and dropped. It landed next to the pathetic cross Sweetwater Eddie had made. I stared, unblinking, at the cross and the weapon for a long time. I knew beyond any doubt that Zeb and I would account in blood for the lives we'd taken. I couldn't control that fact any more than I could command the sun not to rise. It was merely a matter of time and place. But damn it, so be it, I thought. There was an anger welling in me—anger I couldn't actually understand or focus, anger that needed to be released.

"I'll pay my dues," I said aloud, "and I'll die when the time comes. But I'll pay the dues as the partner of Zeb Stone, shootist, not as a damned drunk that kids cover with manure as he lies passed out in an alley. That man—the drunk—was as dead as Sweetwater Eddie. And, if for nothing else, I had Zeb Stone to thank for that. I'd lived more in the period of time since I'd trotted out to meet him on Main Street in Burnt Rock than I had in all my previous years. My Smith & Wesson was resting on the slicker with the other weapons. I leaned over and picked it up, checked its load, and slid it into my holster.

Although I was still very tired, I knew I couldn't sleep. I rolled a cigarette and leaned back against the cool soil of the cave wall and waited for my partner to return.

I pulled the ashes and dead embers out of the long-dead fire, arranged kindling and a few pieces of dry wood, and had a pot of good, double-strength coffee gurgling over red coals by the time Zeb pushed his way into our hideout. He carried the cleaned and gutted carcasses of two large rabbits in one hand and a bunch of wild onions in the other. He sniffed appreciatively.

"That coffee sure does smell good," he said. I poured him a cup. He dropped the rabbits on the slicker and sat next to them, sipping at his coffee. He winced and set the cup down.

"Damn," he said.

"Something wrong with the coffee, Zeb?"

"No—it ain't the coffee. It's just that when anything hot or cold hits where my front grinders was, it hurts like hell. You was knocked out, I guess, but two or three of them posse men laid into me with their boots after they got me tied up. I must have had my yap open, 'cause a boot toe cleaned out my lowers, but my uppers is fine."

"Let me see," I said.

Zeb leaned toward me, his mouth wide open. The fire cast enough light for me to see what I was looking for. The remains of five smashed and broken teeth poked up in shards and points from the dull-gray, lifeless-looking gums in the lower front of his mouth. His breath smelled much like rotting meat, and from the looks of his gums, that odor fit the situation quite well.

"Zeb," I said, "those pieces have to be pulled. I'm pretty sure your gums are already infected, but if we get the remains of the teeth out, you'll probably be okay."

"Damn," Stone grumbled, "if it ain't one thing, it's another. First ol' Sweet goes loony and has to be plugged, an' now my teeth are all busted up. What can I do? There ain't no sawbones nor no dentists around here, that's for damned sure."

"I can take care of it for you," I said. "Is there any whiskey left?"

"Yeah," Zeb said. "We got a full bottle an' maybe half of of another from the posse's gear."

"Good. Drink the half-bottle and we'll get to it."

Zeb fetched the bottle from a pile of equipment near the front of the cave and came back to the fire. He sat, took a long swallow, and lowered the bottle. He wiggled the stump of a tooth, cringed, and drank again. After repeating that sequence five or six times, he was as anesthetized as he could be without falling over or passing out.

I yanked the teeth—or, rather, what was left of the teeth—as quickly as possible. Still, the procedure took a half an hour. The only tools I had were my thumb and forefinger. I had to rock and wiggle most of the chunks of enamel free and then dig and prod around to make sure I'd gotten the roots.

"Thishh ish killin' me, Pound," Zeb slurred from around my fingers in his mouth. "Quit your shhrewin' 'roun' an' get outta my yap!"

When I was satisfied I'd gotten everything that had remained of the teeth, I allowed the gums to bleed a bit in order to let the blood carry out what infection it could. I stopped the bleeding with pressure and a little ball of cloth I'd torn from Zeb's shirt. When the empty sockets seemed relatively dry, I poured whiskey into them. Stone winced and groaned but didn't pull away.

"All set, Zeb," I said.

"Sure," he growled, "just like Colonel Custer was all set at the Little Bighorn." He poured a cup of booze and tilted his head as far back as he could, thus enabling him to dump the whiskey down his craw while completely bypassing the lower front of his mouth.

"You cook an' eat them rabbits," he said. "I sure ain't hungry after you damn near set up housekeeping in my mouth. I'm gonna finish this here bottle an' then lay into the other one if I need to. I couldn't eat nothin' even if I wanted to."

185

Zeb put a sizable dent in the second bottle and then passed out. I added wood to the fire, made a fresh pot of coffee, and broiled the rabbits on sticks over the flames. I ate them both. They were delicious.

I sat drinking coffee and smoking a cigarette. My eyes kept returning to the bottle next to Zeb's prostrate form. It wasn't that I particularly wanted a drink. Or perhaps I did *want* one but knew I wasn't going to take one. The booze was making me uncomfortable. I stared at the bottle until my cigarette was too short to hold and, ultimately, sighed and got to my feet. I picked up the bottle, allowed myself a sniff at the open neck, and dumped the whiskey onto the fire. Blue flames rose through the hissing as the liquid hit the coals. Then both the fire and I settled down. I gnawed at some scraps of rabbit, drank some more coffee, and went to sleep.

There was a six-inch-long lump on the side of my head. I poked at it gingerly the next morning. Sweet's fish-line sutures were holding well. I stood too quickly and experienced only mild dizziness and buzzing in my ears. I wasn't completely sure that I'd had an actual concussion, but whatever I had was bad enough. Either way, I was mending.

In a couple of days, I'd be more than ready for Silver Ridge and Paris.

Chapter Eleven

We rode away from Sweetwater Eddie's safe place on a cloudless, delightfully cool morning. Our mounts, after a week of doing nothing but grazing, were antsy, tugging at their bits, snorting, snapping their hooves from the ground almost before their shoes made contact, much like parade horses or circus ponies.

"Damn," Zeb said, "these two are as nervous as the James brothers in a church." His Appaloosa shied, eyes wide, at some nameless terror that probably didn't exist. My mare crow-hopped and shook her head violently.

"Pound," Zeb asked, "are you a man who'll make a bet on somethin'? Like, say, a horse race?"

I looked over at Zeb, meeting his broad smile with one of my own. "I am," I said. "I am."

"How much, then?"

"I fail to see what difference it makes, Zeb," I answered. "You're flat broke. If that horse runs the way you play poker, I could beat you on foot."

"I ain't gonna be broke after Silver Ridge, though. An' I'll tell you somethin': I ain't about to argue with this jughead all day. The damn fool wants to run, an' the only way he's goin' to behave is to let him gallop out some of his craziness. Same with that mare of yours."

"I need odds," I said.

"Odds, my foot, Pound. That mare looks like she can up an' outrun a slug from a .45. 'Course, if you're scared to run a horse 'cause you took a little spill a few days back, well . . ."

"How far," I asked, "and how much?"

"A thousand," Zeb said. "See that cactus way the hell an' gone—by them rocks?"

I looked in the direction Zeb pointed. "Yes, I see it," I lied. My vision was average at best, but Zeb had the eyes of a hungry hawk. I'd found that trying to convince him that I couldn't see what was so clear to him was a waste of time.

"On three," he said. "First horse past the cactus wins the pot."

I nodded.

We held our horses as still as they allowed. Zeb was on my right side. He began the count. I was far more interested in what his left boot—and spur— were doing than I was in his shouting of numbers.

"One." He bellowed, which didn't make much sense, since I was only a couple of feet away from him. His heel dropped a full inch and he bent forward slightly at the waist.

"Two." Zeb angled his boot. His spur was perhaps an inch from the Appaloosa's side.

I heard Zeb take a long, deep breath. "Thh . . ." he began, concurrently jabbing his horse with his spurs. I was the slightest bit quicker. As soon as I saw his boot move, I threw all my slack rein to my mare and thumped her with my heels. She hurled herself forward as Zeb spurred his Appaloosa. He yelled something that I missed as I took the lead by a full, long stride. I had little—perhaps no—control over the mare. I'd pointed her in the right direction and hoped that she wouldn't veer or swerve.

The sheer, animal joy of the two stretched and galloping horses was intoxicating, exhilarating. The cool air became brisk as it slapped at my face and blurred my vision with tears. I leaned far forward, my chin slightly above my mare's neck. Everything—the heady scent of horse and leather, the crystal clarity of the air, the arrhythmic, frenzied pounding of eight hooves, and my virile, almost insolent acceptance of Zeb's challenge—combined in my mind and battered my senses, and I can very clearly recall thinking that never again would I be this happy, this free, this alive.

I could see the cactus. Zeb's Appaloosa gained some ground, but my mare still led by a full length. I banged my heels into her sides and shrieked into her ear, and she gave me everything she had to give. The cactus was a hundred yards ahead. Very suddenly, Zeb's horse swallowed most of my lead. The Appaloosa's head, nostrils flared and startingly pink inside, ears laid back as if in anger, was at my right boot. I screamed at my mare again. I wanted to win this race more than I ever wanted anything.

Zeb gained a quick six inches, and then another six. We were side by side, perfectly matched, perfectly in stride.

The cactus hurtled toward us. I raised the ends of my reins, leaned even farther forward, and began the motion to lash at the mare's neck. I never completed the move. I could no more punish—cause pain—to this horse that was running her heart out for me than I could gun down my own partner.

Zeb's horse dropped back a foot far more rapidly than he'd gained it. The breathing I heard behind me seemed more labored, less regular. The cactus was ten feet ahead—and then it was twenty feet to the rear. I'd won the race by half a horse length.

I was speechless.

Zeb and I reined to a lope and then to a fast walk. Zeb yelled a long rebel whoop and pounded on my back with his fist.

"Dammit, pard, what a horse race!" he yelled.

I stretched my arm around Zeb's far shoulder and pulled him to me in a clumsy embrace. His smile was as wide as the Mississippi River.

"Damn," he said, "that was a hell of a race, wasn't it, Pound?"

"The best, Zeb," I said. "The best."

We walked the horses in silence until their breathing was normal. Then we stopped and wiped the foam from their chests and sides with our bandannas. Zeb checked his saddlebags and made sure that Sweet's buffalo rifle, which was tied over Zeb's slicker with latigo, hadn't shifted during the race. I was carrying a Winchester 30.06 in the same manner.

We each had three pistols in our gear, other than those in our holsters. My equipment was secure, as was Zeb's.

"How far to Silver Ridge?" I asked.

Stone scratched his head, thinking. "Close as I can figure, maybe a day—day an' a half."

"Are we going to ride all night?"

"Nope. See, we'll need the horses to be fresh to make Paris after we do Silver Ridge. We got to cut these beards off, too. Our descriptions are probably all over the damn state by now, an' them who seen us last seen us with beards. You got a razor, ain't you?"

"I have a razor," I said, "but I don't have a strop or mug or brush. Or soap, for that matter."

"We'll make do," Zeb said. "We'll pull in at the first water we hit, come sundown or thereabouts. Be nice to find some grazin', too."

"You know," I said, "I'll be a bit sorry to shave. I've grown fond of my beard. I think it gives me—well, a distinguished look. Cultured, maybe."

"Yeah," Zeb said, "like a armpit. An' that scar on your melon's right pretty, too."

We rode at an easy pace the rest of the day, rarely moving faster than a lope. We didn't find water until we were well into the night. There was a full moon, which cast enough light so that travel was as safe as it had been at noon. We let the horses drink and then hobbled them. Although there was some scrub grass, it was brittle-dry, and the animals picked at it with little interest.

We built a small fire from stalks, scrub, and twigs, heated a pot of coffee, and then stamped out the embers. Zeb and I split a large can of peaches in heavy syrup Stone had found in Sweet's belongings, and we each had a handful of dusty, rock-hard biscuits Zeb had baked the first day at the cave.

Stone cursed and complained heatedly as he tried to gnaw on what seemed to be near-petrified lumps of dough. Finally, he tossed the biscuits over his shoulder out into the darkness.

"I can't eat them things," he said. "I can mash 'em up with my back teeth, but I can't tear into 'em without no lower front choppers. Damn. I'm gonna get me some of them false grinders I seen in the Sears catalog. You ever know anybody who had those?"

I gave that some thought. "No, I don't believe I have. I think you'd be better off getting false teeth from a dentist, Zeb. The fit will be right."

"Yeah," Zeb said. "I suppose that's real important. See, I'm worried 'bout the damned things fallin' outta my yap. I'd feel like a fool if I was talkin' to somebody an' my teeth fell out. Well, what say we get rid of these beards?"

I fetched my razor from my saddlebags and we wet our faces at the water hole. The blade wasn't particularly well honed. In fact, as Zeb pointed out, it was about as sharp as a horse apple. Still, with considerable effort, pain, bloodshed, and extremely imaginative cursing, we were able to slice, chop, and scrape the beards from our faces.

When the first signs of the sun showed the next morning, Stone and I had already split a pot of coffee and were saddling up for the day's ride.

"We can take it easy today," Zeb said. "We'll camp

four or five miles outta Silver Ridge an' take the bank tomorrow mornin'. After that, ridin' hard, we should make Paris in four hours or so. Problem is, we'll have to steal a couple horses before we tap the Paris bank. See, we need to get to Waco in a big hurry, an' these two couldn't give us the speed we need after the run from Silver Ridge. It's too bad. They're good horses."

"Why don't we buy horses in Paris and then hit the bank?"

"Takes too long. It's lots quicker to gag an' tie a fella or two an' take the best horses we see."

"Suppose," I asked, "we rest a couple of days and then take Silver Ridge and then Paris?"

"Damn, Pound, you still don't see what's goin' on. First off, the horses will be wore out by the ride from Silver Ridge to Paris no matter how long we rest 'em. An' you got to get into your head that we can't *never* rest 'lessen we're in a big town like Houston or Waco. We got a passel of money on our heads, an' we've gunned enough folks to start a small town. Nossir, there ain't a way in the world we can stop."

"Killing or riding?" I was immediately sorry I'd asked that.

Zeb, his back to me, rubbed the Appaloosa's muzzle. After a long, uncomfortable silence, he said quietly, "Neither, Pound. You know that just as good as I do."

It was another rare, temperate day with no wind and clear visibility to the horizon all the way around the compass. The sun, warm and sensual rather than hot and debilitating, was an ally rather than an enemy. We cut good water twice. The second time, we let the horses graze for an hour as we sat and smoked.

Stone blew a perfect smoke ring into the still air. We both watched as the circle became an oval, lengthened, and finally meshed with itself and disappeared.

"That was pretty," Zeb said. "It's what the Indians call a omen. See, if a brave sees hisself a omen—a good one—it means his luck will be good."

"Oh?"

"Sure," Zeb continued. "If he's goin' huntin' he'll do good, an' if he's headed for a battle he'll wallop hell outta his enemies an' not get hurt. We got us a good omen. We'll ride into Waco with so much money we'll need a farm wagon to haul it. You wait an' see if we don't."

We stopped for the night at a good-sized water hole that had patches of still-green, knee-high buffalo grass around it. As we removed our saddles, Zeb untied the Sharps and raised it to his shoulder. He hesitated for a moment, drew a tight bead, and fired. He handed the rifle to me.

"Rabbit for dinner tonight," he said. "See what that omen's doin' for us?"

Zeb walked out on the prairie about seventy-five yards and trotted back carrying roughly half of a large jackrabbit. The slug from the Sharps had taken the other half for itself.

Zeb figured he had little to worry about, camping so close to Silver Ridge. As he put it, "A outlaw'd have to be a damn fool to be settin' at a fire eatin' rabbit so near a town."

I had to agree with him. There was a certain perverse logic in what he said. Killers on the run simply don't make camp when there's daylight left, nor do they build a smoky little fire that points to them like a finger in the sky. We did all three things. Thus, we were drifters or cowhands—innocent and consequently unafraid men—not robbers or killers.

Before dark, Stone checked the shoes of the horses and rubbed the animals down with handsful of buffalo grass. He then let them drink again and hobbled them. We broiled the rabbit, drank two pots of strong coffee, and stretched out to sleep. The tearing of the grass and the slow, grinding, chewing sounds of the horses grazing had the same effect on me that waves or rushing water have on many others. I slept soundly, dreamlessly, until dawn. I came awake to the whirring of the chamber of Zeb's Colt as he checked his load. The morning was cool and clear: The day promised to be a repeat of the one before.

We walked our horses the few miles to Silver Ridge. A hundred yards from the town itself we passed a large, hand-lettered shingle nailed to a post. It read:

TOWN OF SILVER RIDGE
leeve guns—rifels—knifes
at sheriffs offise or
pay $50 and jail

The sign was riddled with various-sized holes ranging from specks of embedded buckshot to clean punctures of slugs from .45s and other handguns. There were three wide, splintery rents through which sunlight passed, making neat, precise designs on the sandy soil.

"A buffalo gun done that," Zeb said. "If they'd been them soft-nosed loads, the first hit woulda took that sign an' flang it from here to California."

I let the "flang" go by. I wasn't in the mood to discuss language with Zeb. I wanted to hit the Silver Ridge bank and pull for Paris.

The town had absolutely nothing about it to distinguish it from Burnt Rock or Morgansville or any other of the hamlets we'd ridden through. Most of the structures were false-fronted: They looked straight and true from the center of the street, but from the side or the rear it was apparent that they were sloppily constructed, weather-tired, single-story buildings crying for paint or whitewash. The bank was in the middle of the block. Smoke rose straight into the sky from the chimney of a restaurant. There were three horses tied to the café's hitching rail. A thin, stoop-shouldered old man was sweeping the dust and dirt out of his general store through the open doorway and into the street. The vibrant clang of a blacksmith's hammer striking good steel rang like a fine bell throughout town. Two cowhands—both with monumental hangovers, from the looks of them—were tying their mounts to the rail in front of the saloon.

"Pound, take a look at *that*," Zeb said in an almost reverent tone of voice. He nodded toward a black horse being led out of the stable and into the sun by a boy of ten or twelve.

"Damn it, Zeb," I snapped, "we're not here to—"

"He's purely beautiful," Zeb continued, as if I hadn't spoken. "I bet he can *fly*. Lookit the legs on him. He's gotta be one-hundred-percent Thoroughbred. I'll tell you this: That horse is probably worth more'n this whole pissant town. Damn—he's a stud horse, too. Lookit the clangers on him. A man could make a awful lot of money in a short time runnin' a firecracker like him against—"

"Stop it, Zeb! I'm nervous enough. Let's do what we came here to do and get out of town. Can't you see this isn't the time to discuss horses?"

"Testy today, ain't you?" Zeb grumbled, as we turned from the middle of the street toward the Silver Ridge Trust Company. We dismounted, looped our reins loosely over the rail, and walked to the open front door of the bank. I checked the street once again. The two cowhands had made it into the saloon. The storekeeper had finished his sweeping and was no longer in his doorway. The only signs of life were a little girl dragging a nondescript-looking puppy behind her by a piece of rope around its neck, and a bushy-haired gentleman driving a farm wagon loaded with bales of hay to the stable where we'd seen the black horse. The boy and the Thoroughbred had apparently gone back into the stall area.

I followed Zeb into the bank, a stride behind him. I pulled the door closed. A teller at the first of three windows didn't look up.

"I'll be with you in a moment," he said, counting bills onto a neat pile in front of him.

"We ain't got the time to wait," Stone said, "this here's a robbery. Don't do nothin' dumb an' you'll stay alive." He had his Colt leveled at the teller. My pistol was in my hand as I pushed through the gate in the little wooden fence that separated the teller's cages and the two offices from the public. The first office was empty. In the second, a young man was adjusting his green eyeshade and another gentleman—older, with much more gray in his hair—was seated behind a large, highly polished desk, holding a match to a cigar.

"Good morning," I said. "We're robbing your bank. Get your hands up and act sensibly and no one will be hurt—but we'll kill you if we have to. Remember that." Their eyes, wide with both surprise and fear, flicked from my gun to my face and back to my gun. The teller raised his hands high and backed toward the wall. The older fellow dropped his cigar as he lifted his hands above his shoulders.

"Out in front," I said, "fast. I get very nervous when my clients move too slowly." Both men hurried from the office to the space behind the teller's cages. The fellow who'd told us to wait was stuffing money into a sack. Zeb was positioned so that he could watch both the front door and the teller. The massive steel safe was gaping open.

"Pack the cash from the safe into a bag," I ordered. The younger man dropped to his knees and began shoving banded sheaves of bills into a cloth sack with the bank's name stenciled on it. The older fellow glared at me. "Come on, old man!" I snarled. "Move!" He lowered himself to his knees with a grunt and reached into the safe.

"Pound!" Zeb called. "Watch him! He might have . . ."

Sunlight streaming through the meticulously clean front windows glinted on the barrel of a derringer as the old man swung it toward me. I fired twice, instinctively, without conscious thought. Both slugs took the banker in the chest, throwing him into the safe. Only the lower half of his body was visible. It was as if the safe were a giant beast of some horrible type, about to crush its victim between its steel jaws. The teller cringed, face chalky white. I grabbed the bag of cash from him.

"Come on, Pound," Zeb ordered. I backed away, still covering the young man with my Smith & Wesson. Stone opened the door and glanced up and down the street.

"Clear!" he shouted. "Let's go!"

We were mounted and at a gallop down Main Street before heads began poking out of windows and from behind doors, their attention drawn by the two reports of my pistol. Stone put three shots into the air to keep the gawkers inside, where they belonged.

We ran our horses a couple of miles outside of Silver Ridge and then reined down to a lope. "Damn," Zeb shouted, "that bank sure had a slew of money in it for such a sorry excuse for a town!" He signaled for a walk. We let our horses suck air, and stuffed money into our saddlebags. I poked the empties out of my pistol and reloaded. Zeb did the same.

"You think you croaked the ol' fella?" Stone asked.

"I don't know. I hit him twice. I had no alternative, Zeb: The old fool was pulling a gun out of the safe."

Zeb nodded. "Yeah," he said. "I seen that. He shoulda done like you said. Ol' goat. You'd think a damn banker would know better'n to draw down on a couple of outlaws. Could be he ain't dead."

I shook my head. "I doubt it," I said. "I doubt it."

Stone dismissed the subject. "We're gonna have to hurt these horses a little, but we got no choice. He spurred the Appaloosa into a lope. I followed. Both animals had plenty of heart. We stretched the gallop as far as we dared, and we walked only to let them gulp enough air to run again.

After three hours—and perhaps a bit longer—of hard riding, we were forced to slow our pace. Entering Paris on a couple of horses with lather-covered chests and taking each stride as if it would be their last would call as much attention to us as if we'd marched into town following a brass band. Folks don't mistreat good horses in Texas.

"We ain't too far out," Zeb said. "What we need to do is hit the stable first an' grab a couple horses. If our luck runs good, there won't be but one or two fellas at the stable. We can tie an' gag 'em in a hurry. The bank won't take long, an' then we dig for Waco."

"What if Paris doesn't have a stable?"

"Pound," Zeb answered, "lemme ask you a question: Do you figure the ranch hands an' cowboys work stock from on foot? An' do the sodbusters have their *women* pull their wagons an' buggies to church on Sunday? Damn, pard, you got to think 'fore you start jawin'."

Zeb untied his bandanna and wiped his face with it. "Now me," he went on, "I'm pretty much used to your ways an' dumb questions an' such. But if you was to start in on a man who don't know you, well, he'd just naturally—"

"Zeb," I interrupted.

"Yeah?"

"Shut the hell up."

"Sure, Pound. I didn't mean nothin'. I was just tryin' to help."

"Don't."

"Sure," he repeated. "But there's no reason to get all fired up. Damn."

We rode on in blessed silence.

By the time we could see Paris, we'd wiped the foam from our horses and they were both moving normally, not dragging their toes as they had been.

"See that fencin' back of that barn toward the far end of town?" Zeb asked.

"Yes," I lied.

"That there's the stable."

"Fine," I said.

Zeb rolled a cigarette as we entered the mouth of Main Street. Horses were tied here and there in town: several in front of the saloon, two at the grain mill, and a buggy and a saddle horse at the general store. Nothing seemed to be moving in Paris, and, oddly enough, there was no one on the street. A yippy, cross-bred dog circled us twice, barking his fool lungs out. When he saw our horses paid no attention to him, the dog trotted back to the alley between the bank and a furniture and undertaking operation and flopped down in the shade.

"Ain't a bad li'l town," Zeb said.

I didn't answer. We rode on at a walk. Stone flipped the nub of his cigarette off to one side and grinned at me.

"I guess our omen's . . . damn! Look there!" Zeb pointed at a black Thoroughbred horse that stood, head hanging, sweat dripping from his chest and sides, in front of a one-story building with a sign that read "Sheriff." Stone buried his spurs in his Appaloosa's sides and drew his Colt. "It's a setup! They figured out what we was up to an' they're layin' for us! We got to—"

Gunfire erupted from everywhere: windows, doorways, rooftops. Zeb hauled his horse around and dropped a man with a rifle to his shoulder in a doorway. I dragged my mare to the left and fired at a pair of men on the roof of the saloon.

"The whole damn town's shootin' at us!" Zeb yelled.

We circled our horses furiously, looking for a way out of the deadly cross fire. A slug tore a hole through my saddle horn, ripping the stretched rawhide and splintering the hardwood beneath it. I leveled my pistol at a man in a restaurant window who was poking a rifle barrel through the glass. The glass shattered and the face disappeared in a red mist. I fired at a rifleman on a roof and missed. Bullets buzzed past me. Glass was crashing and shattering nonstop, and the gunfire at us became even more intense. Stone fumbled his Sharps loose and blasted a huge hole through a man in a gunfighter's crouch in front of a dress shop. I took down a fat, jowly man who was swinging a shotgun toward Zeb. The roar of the Sharps sounded at my side. My horse screamed and staggered drunkenly, blood rushing from her nostrils. Zeb was next to me. I grabbed his shoulders and swung onto the Appaloosa behind him. A cowhand fired from an alley. I squeezed my trigger and the hammer clicked uselessly, futilely, against spent cartridges. Stone levered the Sharps and blew a sniper from a rooftop.

"Hold on, Pound!" Zeb shouted, spurring hard. We approached the general store from a slight angle at a full gallop. We smashed through the plate-glass window into the store with a tremendous, crashing impact that sprayed the interior of the mercantile with a storm of shards and larger pieces of jagged, deadly-sharp glass. The horse wedged a leg between two plows and went down, the gut-wrenching snap of the bones louder than the gunfire that followed us through the window. Zeb hit the floor rolling toward a pile of crates at the rear of the store. A gray-haired lady—either an employee or a customer—stood holding a sack of soda crackers, frozen, unable to move. Stone got his feet under him and tackled the woman, dragging her behind the crates with him. I went off the right side of the Appaloosa and hit the floor hard enough to slam the wind out of me. Gasping for air, I scrambled behind a display case and some crates at the back of the long rectangle of the store. The shipping and receiving door was directly behind me. It was secured with a pair of hasp locks at the top and bottom and a wide beam across the center.

Gunfire from the street dwindled and then stopped.

Zeb, about ten feet to my left, was sitting on the face-down woman's back. The pitiful moaning of the horse rose in pitch until it was a shriek. Stone said something to the woman, rose, and fired the Sharps. The horse was silent.

I looked around. To my right was a glass-fronted display case of hand tools. I was crouched behind a large wooden shipping box stenciled "Farm Implements." The horse had taken out just about all of the window and we had a good view of the street.

"Pound," Zeb called.

"Yes?"

"You hit?"

"No. Are you?"

"Yeah. Damn. Twice: my left shoulder an' elbow. My arm ain't worth nothin'. You got anything other'n your pistol?"

"No."

"Well, damn, Pound, crawl on up there an' grab a couple of them Winchesters an' all the ammo you can carry 'fore them sneaky hounds out there figure out they got us trapped. I got to hold down this lady."

A display of eight or ten Winchester .44-caliber rifles had been smashed open by the falling, writhing horse. I edged toward them in a deep crouch. I threw the two rifles closest to me back to my crate and tossed boxes of shells in the same direction as rapidly as I could pick them up. A bullet gouged a deep hole in the floor next to me. I hustled awkwardly, still crouched, to my cover.

"Zeb?"

"Yeah?"

"I'm going to slide a rifle over. There's too much open space between for me to get to you without being blown to hell."

"Yeah," Stone answered. "Keep behind your cover."

I shoved a rifle across the ten or so feet of floor that separated us. The Winchester banged into the side of Zeb's crate. He reached out, groped for a moment, found the stock, and pulled the rifle back behind his cover with him. I lofted three boxes of bullets to him. We both loaded our handguns from shells in our gunbelts, then did the same with the rifles and .44-caliber ammunition.

"Let the woman go," a voice from the street shouted, "an' we'll take you boys alive. There's been enough killin' here today."

Zeb fired several shots in the general direction of the voice. "Don't you go givin' me no orders," Stone hollered. "I'm right up on top of the heap an' you cowardly hounds know it. I got the lady. An' when I come out, she's comin' with me. My partner's losin' blood by the damn bucket. Let him croak in peace."

"Maybe our doc can fix your friend."

"An' maybe hogs fly with crows," Zeb responded.

I watched as Stone wrapped lengths of heavy, coarse twine from a spool next to him around the woman's wrists and ankles. He cut the sections of cord with his pocketknife. His left arm was useless, and blood was puddling and seeping out from around his crate. He could grasp with his fingers, but he had to position his left arm with his right hand.

He reached under the lady's dress and pulled at some cloth. Her bloomers came away with a ripping sound. He fashioned a gag from the underwear and tugged the clumsily assembled knot tight with his good hand.

"Pound," he called, "start shootin' out the front of the store to cover me."

I worked the smooth, tight lever of the Winchester and fired eight or ten rounds toward the street. Stone hustled to a display case near the front door, grabbed something, and ran for his cover.

"Damn," he grunted, as if his mouth were full.

"What did you go after, Zeb?"

"Licorice whips."

"What?!"

"Licorice whips. I've been kinda partial to 'em since I was a kid. Want me to toss you a few? I got the whole jar, so I got plenty to share."

"Why in the name of all that's good and holy," I asked, "do you do this type of thing to me? Here we are, about to die in a general store in a crummy little town no one has ever heard of, and you offer me licorice whips. You're crazy, Zeb. I mean it: You're insane."

"You coulda just said 'no' without all that other stuff," Zeb muttered. "An' keep your voice down— you're supposed to be dyin' or dead. Now listen: You crawl over there an' get one of them dresses an' put it on."

"Zeb . . ."

Stone's voice turned suddenly cold and businesslike. "Do like I say, Pound. Far's I can see, we ain't got but one chance, an' we're goin' to give it a go. I ain't gonna be gunned down in no general store if I can help it."

I slithered on my belly to a rack of gowns, pulled one to the floor, and crawled back to my cover.

"Grab one of them sunbonnets, too," Zeb ordered. I did as I was told.

"Hey, out there!" Zeb yelled.

"Whatd' ya want, killer?"

"Here's how it's gonna go," Stone answered. "I want two rested, saddled horses out in front in ten minutes. Don't try slippin' me no plugs, neither. I've forgot more about horses than you sodbusters an' storekeeps'll ever know. I'll let the lady go outside of town a few miles. Then you boys can do your damndest. You already killed my pard. I got nothin' to lose. I'll hang if you don't kill me. But I'll tell you this: I'm gonna take a whole passel of you right along with me to hell. Now, get them horses!"

"We'll get them," a voice from the street answered.

I began pulling the gown over my head. Fortunately, it had full, long sleeves and was wide enough to fit over my hips. I put the sunbonnet on my head and tied the drawstring under my chin.

"Can we make it, Zeb?" I called over quietly.

There was a long period of silence as Stone deliberated. I could hear snatches of conversation from the street. The voices seemed louder, more angry, than they had a few moments ago.

"Zeb?"

"I heard you, Pound. I was thinkin' on it. No. We probably can't make it. There's nothin' to stop us from tryin', though. Hell, I'd rather get shot than hang anyways, wouldn't you?"

I thought it over. "I suppose so," I answered.

"Hey, outlaw!" a man out front called. "We got the horses. We'll stand back. But if you hurt the lady, we'll cut you to bits. Understand?"

"Come on, pard," Zeb said. "Let me put my left arm over your shoulders so's it looks like I'm holdin' on to you to keep you from runnin'."

"How do we mount, Zeb? They'll shoot hell out of you as soon as we're on separate horses."

"Not if I'm holdin' my Colt against your head—or real close to it—they won't." Zeb smiled. "You don't look half bad in that dress an' bonnet," he said.

Zeb's left arm was gushing blood. He used his right hand to hang it over my shoulders. He drew his pistol, pointed it at my face, and we walked side by side through the carnage in the store. Two saddled horse, reins hanging in the dust, eyed us suspiciously as we approached them.

"I got a real light trigger on this Colt," Zeb shouted as we stepped outside. "One of you even looks at me wrong an' this here lady is dead."

"I'll get up first an' keep my gun on you," Zeb whispered to me. "You climb on real slow an' clumsy like you ain't used to—"

A voice slashed through the tense, still air like the first stroke of lightning announcing a violent storm.

"That ain't no lady! Lookit them boots!"

Zeb shoved me backward. My heel caught in the dress and I went down. Zeb swung his pistol toward the voice. Two slugs tore out through the back of his shirt. He took a step forward and attempted to raise his Colt. Then, still standing, he began to jerk this way and that as the combined forces of the town of Paris, Texas, opened fire on him with shotguns, pistols, rifles, and buffalo guns. Even after he was down, the shooting continued, making his dead body jump and twitch in the blood-spattered dust and grit of the street. Men were shouting, yelling, pumping round after round into Zeb's body. I began to push myself to my feet when something crashed into my skull from behind.

"So. That's about it, boy—the whole story. The fellow who bashed me with the ax handle could just as easily have shot me. I suspect that the dress and the fact that I was already down had something to do with it."

The young man's eyes hadn't left my face throughout the entire narrative. "You and Mr. Stone were the best," he said, "even better'n the James brothers. Wait 'til I tell my friends I was right in the same cell with you." There was a large, livid bruise across the young fellow's forehead. Both his eyes were blackened, and his lips were lacerated and swollen.

"Remember what I told you about your trial, boy," I said. "Tell them that the girl—Hannah, wasn't it?— lured you into the barn and asked you for money to perform the act in which her father caught you. That's very important."

"Yessir. It don't make no sense, though. I didn't

rape no statue. Hell, I never even *seen* a statue, 'cept in pictures."

I sighed. "Forget about statutory rape. It's merely the name of the charge for which you were arrested. It has nothing whatsoever to do with statues. Just remember what I've told you."

"Yessir. I sure will." He touched his face gingerly and winced in pain. "I'll tell you one thing, Mr. Taylor: I ain't never going to statuate the daughter of a blacksmith again. That man had fists on him the size of a full-growed hog's head." The boy hesitated for a moment. "I'm awful sorry you're going to swing tomorrow, Mr. Taylor."

"So am I, Dave," I said. "So am I."

We heard voices from the front of the jail, in the sheriff's office:

"You would dare search a man of the cloth for a weapon? Know ye not that the Bible is far more powerful than any earthly device for death?"

"Sorry, Reverend, them's the rules. Everybody gets searched," the sheriff said. "You'd best do your soul-saving in a hurry. It's after midnight, and Taylor hangs at dawn."

The door between the office and the single cell swung open. "Taylor," the sheriff said, "there's a preacher here who says he was sent by your kin."

A tall, muscularly built man with silver hair that encircled his head like a halo strode down the corridor to our cell. He was dressed in the standard, black preacher's garb. He held a Bible in his right hand. Even in the wavering, unsteady light of the lantern hung in the aisle, I could see the man was handsome in a rugged, outdoors manner. He walked with a stiff-backed, almost military gait.

"Will you give us no privacy?" the reverend asked.

"Nope."

"God in mysterious ways His miracles works," the preacher said. "Perhaps it's for the best. Lawrence will find far more consolation between the covers of the Good Book than a mere mortal such as I could offer." He handed the Bible to me through the bars. I took it and returned to my cot.

"Have faith, my son," the preacher said.

The sheriff, keys clinking against one another on the short silver chain that hung from his gunbelt, followed the reverend out of the cell area and into his office, pulling the door shut behind him.

I opened the Bible in my lap. The center of the pages had been cut away quite neatly, and in the space was an Army Colt.

"Well," I said. "Well."

There was a note tucked under the barrel of the pistol. I took it out and closed the Bible. The note was in pencil on butcher paper, and the handwriting was not unlike that of my worst students.

I'm Zebs pa. Zebs ma, she taut me the preecher talk. The thing is, ain't nobody going to hang my boys pardner. Theres a waggin jist outside of town with a bunch of crates and sich on it. Theres a good bay horse tyed at the saloon with a white stripe on his mussle so you cant miss him. Lock that fool sheriff in your sell and grab that bay and ride like hell to the wagin and send the bay on his way with a wack. I left good space under all them crates to hide you. Shouldn't be no problems. Don't worry about the horse. Hes stole. Then you and me and Zebs brother can rob some banks and be outlaws just like you and Zeb was.

Sined,
Thaddeus Howard Stone

I looked at the note for a long time before I folded it up and tucked it in my pocket. When I looked up, I saw that the boy had been watching me closely.

"Dave," I asked, "have you done much riding double?"

His grin was enough to light the cell. "You bet I have, Mr. Taylor! Why, me an' my brother, we had to share a horse when we was—"

I held up my hand to silence Dave, and I returned his grin. I opened the Bible and removed the Colt.

"Sheriff," I shouted. "Sheriff!"

NIGHT OF THE
COMANCHEROS
LAURAN PAINE

In these two brilliant novellas, celebrated author Lauran Paine perfectly captures the drama of the frontier and the gritty determination of those who lived there. In "Paid in Blood," an inept Indian agent has put the Apaches on the warpath, and U.S. Army Scout Caleb Doorn is all that stands between the bloodthirsty braves and the white settlers. The title story tells of Buck Baylor, who returns home from his first cattle drive to find his father murdered and the countryside in the unrelenting grip of vicious outlaws. Will Buck be able to avenge his family before he, too, is killed?

Will Henry
THE SCOUT

Will Henry remains one of the most widely recognized and honored novelists ever to write about the American West. As demonstrated by the three novellas in this brilliant collection, throughout his career he was able to create exciting, authentic tales filled with humanity, adventure, and empathy. "Red Blizzard" is the tale of a Pawnee scout caught between the U.S. Army and the Sioux in the time of the wars with Crazy Horse. "Tales of the Texas Rangers" recounts the courageous battle waged by the Rangers against any danger, from Comanches to John Wesley Hardin. The title character in "The Hunkpapa Scout" is a trail guide for a wagon train set upon by rampaging Sioux. He will be the only hope to warn the nearby cavalry troop…if he survives!

- -

Dorchester Publishing Co., Inc.
P.O. Box 6640   ___5568-6
Wayne, PA 19087-8640 $5.99 US/$7.99 CAN

Please add $2.50 for shipping and handling for the first book and $.75 for each additional book. NY and PA residents, add appropriate sales tax. No cash, stamps, or CODs. Canadian orders require an extra $2.00 for shipping and handling and must be paid in U.S. dollars. Prices and availability subject to change. **Payment must accompany all orders.**

Name: _____

Address: _____

City: _____ State: _____ Zip: _____

E-mail: _____

I have enclosed $_____ in payment for the checked book(s).

For more information on these books, check out our website at www.dorchesterpub.com.
_____ *Please send me a free catalog.*

LOUIS L'AMOUR

THE SIXTH SHOTGUN

No writer is associated more closely with the American West than Louis L'Amour. Collected here are two of his most exciting works, in their original forms. The title story, a tale of stagecoach robbery and frontier justice, is finally available in its full-length version. Similarly, the short novel included in this volume, *The Rider of the Ruby Hills*, one of L'Amour's greatest range war novels, was published first in a magazine, then expanded by the author into a longer version years later. Here is a chance to experience the novel as it appeared in its debut, as L'Amour originally wrote it.

Dorchester Publishing Co., Inc.
P.O. Box 6640   ___5580-5
Wayne, PA 19087-8640 $6.99 US/$8.99 CAN

MAX BRAND®

JOKERS EXTRA WILD

Anyone making a living on the rough frontier took a bit of a gamble, but no Western writer knows how to up the ante like Max Brand. In "Speedy—Deputy," the title character racks up big winnings on the roulette wheel, but that won't help him when he's named deputy sheriff—a job where no one's lasted more than a week. "Satan's Gun Rider" continues the adventures of the infamous Sleeper, whose name belies his ability to bury a knife to the hilt with just a flick of his wrist. And in the title story, a professional gambler inherits a ring that lands him in a world of trouble.

Dorchester Publishing Co., Inc.
P.O. Box 6640
Wayne, PA 19087-8640

___-5442-6
$5.99 US/$7.99 CAN

Please add $2.50 for shipping and handling for the first book and $.75 for each additional book. NY and PA residents, add appropriate sales tax. No cash, stamps, or CODs. Canadian orders require an extra $2.00 for shipping and handling and must be paid in U.S. dollars. Prices and availability subject to change. **Payment must accompany all orders.**

Name: _____

Address: _____

City: _____ State:_____ Zip: _____

E-mail: _____

I have enclosed $_____ in payment for the checked book(s).

For more information on these books, check out our website at www.dorchesterpub.com.
____ *Please send me a free catalog.*

COTTON SMITH

DEATH RIDES A RED HORSE

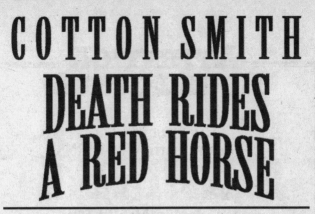

What started as a simple trip for supplies has turned into a race against time and a fight to survive. Cole Kerry almost single-handedly broke up a raid on the town by a gang of outlaws. But one of them grabbed Cole's wife as they rode off, and Cole himself was shot in the back when he tried to track them down. Now it's up to his older brother, Ethan, to find Cole and rescue his wife—if they're still alive. It's a tough enough job for any man. Ethan isn't about to let the fact that he's blind stand between him and what he needs to do.
